SARA MESA is the author of ten works of fiction, including *Scar* (winner of the Ojo Critico Prize), *Four by Four* (a finalist for the Herralde Prize), *An Invisible Fire* (winner of the Premio Málaga de Novela), *Among the Hedges*, *Un Amor*, which was named by several Spanish newspapers as the book of the year for 2020, and, most recently, *La familia*. Her works have been translated into more than ten different languages, and she has been widely praised for her concise, sharp writing style.

KATIE WHITTEMORE translates from the Spanish. Her full-length translations include works by Sara Mesa, Javier Serena, Aroa Moreno Durán, Lara Moreno, Nuria Labari and Katixa Agirre. Forthcoming translations include novels by Jon Bilbao, Juan Gómez Bárcena, Almudena Sánchez, Aliocha Coll and Pilar Adón. She received an NEA Translation Fellowship in 2022 to translate Moreno's *In Case We Lose Power*.

UN AMOR

Sara Mesa

Translated from the Spanish
by Katie Whittemore

PEIRENE

Published in Great Britain in 2024 by
Peirene Press Ltd
The Studio, 10 Palace Yard Mews
Bath BA1 2NH

Originally published in Spanish as *Un amor* by Anagrama
Copyright © 2020 by Sara Mesa
Translation copyright © 2023 by Katie Whittemore

Published by arrangement with Open Letter
Books at the University of Rochester

ISBN: 978-1-908670-97-7

This book is a work of fiction. Names, characters, businesses,
organizations, places and events are either the product of the
author's imagination or used fictitiously. Any resemblance to actual
persons, living or dead, events or locales is entirely coincidental.

Design by Orlando Lloyd
Cover artwork by María Medem
Offset by Tetragon, London
Printed and bound by TJ Books, Padstow, Cornwall

UN AMOR

I

Nightfall is when the weight descends on her, so heavy she has to sit down to catch her breath.

Outside, the silence isn't what she expected. It isn't true silence. There is a distant rumble, like the sound of a motorway, although the closest one is regional and three kilometres away. She hears crickets, too, and barking, a car horn, a neighbour rounding up his livestock.

The sea was nicer, but also more expensive. Out of her reach.

And what if she'd held out a little longer, saved a little more?

She would rather not think. She closes her eyes, slowly sinks into the sofa, half her body hanging off, an unnatural position that will give her a cramp if she doesn't move soon. She realizes this. She lies down as best she can. Dozes.

Better to not think, but the thoughts come and slide through her, intertwining. She tries to release them as soon as they appear, but they accumulate there, one thought on top of another. This effort, this drive to let them go as quickly as they come, is itself a thought too intense for her brain.

When she gets the dog, it will be easier.

When she organizes her things and sets up her desk and tidies the area around the house. When she waters and trims – everything is so dry, so neglected. When it cools down.

It will be much better when the weather cools.

The landlord lives in Petacas, a small town a fifteen-minute drive away. He turns up two hours later than they had agreed. Nat is sweeping the porch when she hears the Jeep. She looks up, squints. The man has parked at the entrance to the property, in the middle of the road, and comes over, shuffling his feet. It's hot. It's noon and already the heat is dry and unpleasant.

He doesn't apologize for being late. He smiles, shaking his head. His lips are thin, his eyes sunken. His worn coverall is splattered with grease stains. It's hard to guess his age. His decline has nothing to do with the years, but rather with his weary expression, the way he swings his arms and bends his knees as he walks. He stops before her, puts his hands on his hips, and looks around.

'Already getting started, eh? How was your night?'

'Fine. Mostly. Too many mosquitoes.'

'You've got a gadget there in the dresser drawer. One of those repellent things.'

'Yeah, but there wasn't any liquid in it.'

'Well, sorry, kid,' he spreads his arms wide. 'Life in the country, eh!'

Nat does not return his smile. A bead of sweat drips from her temple. She wipes it on the back of her hand and, in that gesture, finds the strength she needs to attack.

'The bedroom window doesn't close right and the bathroom tap leaks. Not to mention how dirty everything is. It's a lot worse than I remember.'

The landlord's smile goes cold, gradually disappearing from his face. His jaw tenses as he prepares to reply. Nat senses that he is a man prone to anger and she wishes she could backtrack. Arms crossed, the man contends that she visited the house and was perfectly aware of its condition. If she didn't pay attention to the details, that's her problem, not his. He reminds her that he came down – twice – on the price. And he tells her, lastly, that he will take care of all the necessary repairs himself. Nat isn't sure that's a good idea, but she doesn't argue. Nodding, she wipes away another bead of sweat.

'It's so hot.'

'You going to blame me for that, too?'

The man turns around and calls to the dog that has been scratching around in the dirt near the Jeep.

'How's this one?'

The dog hasn't looked up since it arrived. Skittish, it sniffs the ground, tracking like a hound. It's a long-legged, greyish mutt with an elongated snout and rough coat. Its penis is slightly erect.

'Well, do you like him or not?'

Nat stutters.

'I don't know. Is he a good dog?'

'Sure he's a good dog. He won't win any beauty contests, you can see that for yourself, but you don't care about that, do you? Isn't that what you said, that you didn't care? He doesn't have fleas or anything bad. He's young, he's healthy.

And he doesn't eat much, so you won't have to worry about that. He'll rummage. He takes care of himself.'

'All right,' Nat says.

They go inside the house, review the contract, sign – she, with a careless scribble; he, ceremoniously, pressing the pen firmly to the paper. The landlord has only brought one copy, which he tucks away, assuring her that he'll get hers to her when he can. Doesn't matter, Nat thinks, the contract has no validity whatsoever, even the listed price isn't real. She doesn't bring up the problem with the window or the bathroom tap again. Neither does he. He extends his hand theatrically, narrowing his eyes as he looks at her.

'Better for us to get along, isn't it.'

The dog doesn't seem to notice when the man returns to the Jeep and starts the engine. He stays in the front yard, pacing and sniffing the dry dirt. Nat calls to him, clicks her tongue and whistles, but he shows no sign of obeying.

The landlord hasn't told her the dog's name. If it even has one.

If asked to explain why she was there, she'd be hard pressed to come up with a convincing answer. That's why, when the moment arrives, she hedges and babbles about a change of scenery.

'People must think you're crazy, right?'

The cashier chews gum as she piles Nat's shopping on the counter. It's the only store within a few-mile radius, an establishment with no sign where foodstuffs and hygiene products accumulate in a jumble. Shopping there is expensive and the pickings are slim, but Nat is reluctant to take the car to Petacas. She rummages in her wallet and counts out the notes she needs.

The girl from the shop is in a chatty mood. Brazen, she asks Nat all about her life, making her uncomfortable. The girl wishes she could do what Nat's done, but the opposite, she says. Move to Cárdenas, where stuff actually happens.

'Living here sucks. There aren't even any guys!'

She tells Nat that she used to go to high school in Petacas, but she quit. She doesn't like studying, she's crap at every subject. Now she helps out in the shop. Her mom gets chronic migraines, and her dad also manages the crops, so she helps out by taking care of things at the store. But as soon as she turns eighteen, she's out of there. She could be a cashier in Cárdenas, or a nanny. She's good with kids. The few kids who ever wind up in La Escapa, she adds with a smile.

'This place sucks,' she repeats.

It's the girl who tells Nat about the people who live in the surrounding houses and farms. She tells her about the gypsy family squatting in a dilapidated farmhouse, right by the slip road to the motorway. A bus picks the kids up every morning; they're the only kids who live in La Escapa year-round. And there's the old couple in the yellow house. The woman is some kind of witch, the girl claims. She can predict the future and read your mind.

'It's creepy because she's a little nuts,' she laughs.

She tells Nat about the hippie in the wooden house, and the guy they call 'The German' even though he isn't from Germany, and Gordo's bar – although to call the warehouse where they serve bottles of beer a bar is, she admits, a bit overboard. There are other people who come and go according to the rhythms of the countryside, day-workers hired for two-week stints or for just the day, but also whole families who have inherited houses they can't manage to sell and live somewhere else for half the year. But you never see women on their own. Not women Nat's age, she specifies.

'Old ladies don't count.'

In the first days, Nat gets confused and mixes up all that information, in part because she listened absently, in part because she's in unfamiliar territory. La Escapa's borders are blurry, and even though there is a relatively compact cluster of small houses – right where hers is – other build-ings are scattered further away, some inhabited and others not. From the outside, Nat can't tell whether they are homes or barns, if there are people inside or just livestock. She loses her bearings on the dirt roads and if it weren't for the shop as a point of reference – which sometimes feels more familiar to her than the house she has rented and has been sleeping in for a week – she'd feel lost. The area isn't even pretty, though at sunset, when the edges soften and the light turns golden, she finds a kind of beauty to cling to.

Nat takes her grocery bags and bids goodbye to the girl. But before she exits the shop, she turns and asks about the landlord. Does the girl know him? The girl puckers her lips, shakes her head slowly. No, not really, she says. He's lived in Petacas a long time.

'I do remember seeing him around here when I was little though. He always had a bunch of dogs and a really bad temper. Then he got married, or got together with someone, and left. I guess his wife didn't want to live in La Escapa – can't blame her. This place is worse for girls. Even though Petacas ain't anything special. I wouldn't want to live there either, no way.'

She tries to play with the dog, tossing him an old ball she found in the woodpile, but instead of catching it and bringing it back, the dog limps away. When she crouches beside him, putting herself on his level so he won't be afraid, he slinks off with his tail between his legs. The dog is a piece of work, she thinks, a real rotter. Sieso, they'd call him where she comes from. It seems a good a name as any – after all, she has to call him something. It certainly describes his unpleasant nature. But Sieso is as inscrutable as he is unsociable. He hangs around, but it's like he isn't there at all. Why should she have to settle for a dog like that? Even the little dog in the shop, an extremely anxious chihuahua mix, is much more pleasant. All the dogs she meets on the roads – and there are tons of them – run over when she calls them. A lot of them are looking to be fed, of course, but also petted; they are nosy and curious, wanting to find out who this new girl in the neighbourhood is. Sieso doesn't even seem interested in eating. If she feeds him, great, and if not, that's fine too. The landlord wasn't kidding: the animal's upkeep is cheap. Sometimes Nat is ashamed of the antipathy she feels towards the animal. She asked for a dog and here he is. Now she cannot – must not – say – or even think – that she doesn't want him.

One morning, she meets the hippie in the shop. That's what the girl called him. Now she waits languidly on them both, smoking a cigarette with no sense of urgency. The hippie is a little older than Nat, though he can't be more than forty. Tall and strong, his skin is weathered by the sun and his hands are broad and cracked. His look is firm but placid. He wears his hair long, terribly cut, and his beard is on the reddish side. Why the girl calls him 'hippie' is something Nat has to guess. Maybe it's his long hair or because, like Nat, he is a stranger from the city: something incomprehensible for anyone who has lived in La Escapa since childhood and can only think of escaping. The truth is, the hippie has also lived there a long time. He is, therefore, nothing new, unlike Nat. She observes him out the corner of her eye, his curt, efficient, sure movements. While she waits her turn, she runs her hand over the back of the dog he has with him. She's a chocolate Labrador, old but undeniably elegant. The dog wags her tail and noses Nat's crotch. The three of them laugh.

'What a good girl,' Nat says.

The hippie nods and holds out his hand. Then he changes his mind, withdraws it and moves in to kiss her. Just one kiss on the cheek, which causes Nat to remain with her face tilted, waiting for the second kiss that doesn't come. He tells her his name: Píter. With an i, he specifies: P-í-t-e-r. At least that's how he likes to spell it, except when he's forced to write it officially. The less one writes one's real name, the better, he jokes. It's only good for signing cheques at the bank, for those thieves.

'Natalia,' she introduces herself.

Then comes the obligatory question: what is she doing in La Escapa? He's seen her out on the trails and also saw her tidying up the land around the house. Is she going to live there? Alone? Nat feels awkward. She would prefer not to be watched while she works, especially unawares, but it's inevitable because the bounds of the property are only marked by fine wire mesh, denuded of vegetation. She tells him she's only staying a couple of months.

'I've seen the dog, too. You didn't bring him with you, did you?'

'How do you know?'

Píter confesses that he knows the animal. One of the landlord's many. That dog, in fact, is probably the worst. Her landlord will pick them up from wherever and doesn't train them, doesn't vaccinate them, doesn't take the slightest care of them. He uses and then abandons them. Did she ask for the dog? She can be sure the landlord has given her the most useless of the pack.

Nat considers this and the man suggests she give the dog back. There's no reason to settle if he isn't what she wanted. The landlord isn't a good guy, he says, she'd be better off keeping her distance. He doesn't like to speak badly of anyone, he insists, but the landlord is another matter. Always thinking about how to scam people.

'I can get you a dog if you want.'

The conversation leaves Nat uneasy. Sitting on her doorstep with a lukewarm bottle of beer – the fridge, too, is on the fritz – she watches Sieso sleeping next to the fence, stretched out in the sunshine. The flies loiter on his slightly swollen belly, where blemishes of old wounds are visible.

The thought of returning him is deeply unsettling.

*

The house is a squat structure, single-storey, with windows practically level with the ground and one bedroom with two single beds. Nat wanted the landlord to take away one of the beds – she won't need it – so she could set up a desk instead. She'd be fine with a simple board on four legs. She considers calling him but keeps putting it off. When she sees him – she'll have to see him sooner or later – she will ask. Or hint. For the time being, she'll work without a desk, making do with the only table, which she moves against the wall because the house is gloomy and damp, even during the day. The kitchen – little more than a countertop and hob – is so dingy that she has to turn on the overhead light just to make a cup of coffee. Outside is different. Starting at daybreak, the sun beats down on the land, and working in the yard, even first thing in the morning, is exhausting. She tries hoeing rows to plant peppers, tomatoes, carrots – whatever grows fast and easily. She read about doing it. She's even seen a few videos that explain the process step by step. But once she's in the dirt, she's incapable of putting any of it into practice. She'll have to get over her embarrassment and ask somebody. Maybe Píter.

She sits down in the evening to translate for an hour or two. She can never quite concentrate. Maybe she requires an adaptation period, she tells herself, no need to obsess yet. To clear her head, she takes walks around the surrounding area. No matter how much she calls him, Sieso refuses to accompany her, and so she goes alone, listening to music on her earphones. When she sees someone else approaching, she speeds up and sometimes jogs a bit. She prefers to go unnoticed, not be forced to introduce herself or chat, even if that means pretending to exercise.

Cork oaks, holm oaks and olive trees stud the drought-ridden terrain. The rock-rose, sticky and unassuming, are the only flowers to dot the land. The monotony of the fields is broken up only by the mass of El Glauco, a low mountain of bush and shrub that looks like it's been sketched in charcoal on a naked sky. On El Glauco, it is said, there are still foxes and wild boar, though the hunters who go up only come back with strings of quail and rabbit on their belts. It's a spooky mountain, Nat thinks, quickly dismissing the thought. Why spooky? Glauco is an ugly name, for sure; she supposes it must come from its pale, wan colour. The word glauco reminds her of a diseased eye, with conjunctivitis, or elderly eyes, glassy and red, almost tarnished. She realizes she's letting herself be influenced by the meaning of glaucoma. Coincidentally, the word glauco has appeared in the book she is attempting to translate, as an adjective attributed to the main character, the fearsome father who at a certain point unleashes an injurious imprecation at one of his sons, while he, according to the text, fixes him with a glaucous gaze. At first, Nat thought of an eye infection, but later understood that a glaucous gaze is simply an empty, inexpressive look, the kind in which the pupil appears dead, almost opaque. What, then, is the correct meaning? Light green, blueish green, sickly, dim, distant? She will have to orient the rest of the paragraph around the term she chooses. Opting for a literal translation without understanding the genuine spirit of the sentence would be like cheating.

Despite all her walking and physical labour, she sleeps poorly at night. She doesn't dare open the windows. Not just because of the mosquitoes, which eat her alive despite all the products she bought. She's also found spiders and salamanders inside the house; horrified, she even discovered a centipede in one of her shoes. A different morning, she finds the kitchen overrun with ants because she left food on the counter. During the day, she is besieged by flies, both in and outside the house. Can anything be done? she wonders. Or is this just the country, as her landlord would say? No matter how much she cleans, everything is dirty. She sweeps and sweeps but the dust comes in through the cracks and accumulates in the corners. If she at least had a fan for sleeping, she thinks, she could close the windows and everything would be more comfortable. She would wake up rested and with more energy to clean, translate, and work in the garden – or on her plans for the garden, more like.

She decides to go to Petacas to buy one. While she's at it, she thinks, she might as well get some tools. A hoe, buckets, a shovel, pruning shears, a sieve, and a few other things. She can always figure out the exact names of what she needs.

She knows nothing about tools.

She is surprised by the activity in Petacas. It takes her a while to find parking; the layout of the roads is so chaotic and the signage so contradictory that, once you enter the town, an unexpected detour can easily take you right out of it again. The houses are modest, their façades worse for wear and mostly plain, but there are some brick buildings, too, up to six storeys tall and distributed arbitrarily here and there. The businesses are clustered around the main square; the town hall – an ostentatious building with large eaves and stained-glass windows – is surrounded by small bars and corner shops run by Chinese families selling everything under the sun. Nat buys a small fan at one of them. Then she wanders in search of a hardware store, reluctant to ask for directions. She is struck by the neglected appearance of the women, who go around with dishevelled hair, wearing sandals. Lots of the men – even the old ones – are wearing tank tops. There are just a few children, and they're unsupervised, licking ice lollies, scampering, rolling on the ground. The people – men, women, kids, all loud and sloppy – look strangely alike. Inbreeding, Nat thinks. Her landlord fits in perfectly.

She is worried about running into him, but it's Píter, not the landlord, whom she meets in the hardware store. She is happy to see him: someone she knows, someone friendly, someone finally smiling at her and coming over. What are you doing here, he asks. Nat shows him the box with the fan and he scowls. Why didn't she ask the landlord? It's his responsibility to keep the property in habitable condition. Not air conditioning, of course, but a fan at least.

'Or you could have asked me. That's what neighbours are for.'

Nat looks for an excuse. She's happy to buy one, she says. When she leaves La Escapa, she'll take it with her. He looks at her sideways, pretending not to believe her.

'And what did you come here to buy? Tools to fix everything he left broken?'

21

Nat shakes her head.

'No. Stuff for the garden.'

'You're going to plant a garden?'

'Well, just something basic… Peppers and aubergines, I guess they're easy. I at least want to try.'

Píter takes her by the arm and steps closer.

'Don't buy anything,' he whispers.

He tells her that he can lend her all the tools she needs. He says, too, that she might as well forget the idea of a garden. Nothing's grown on her land in years; the soil is totally depleted; it would take days and days of hard work to get it into shape. If she insists – Nat hangs on that word, insists – he could lend her a hand, but he absolutely advises against it. Although he speaks smoothly, Píter's voice contains indisputable certainty, an expert's confidence. Nat nods, waits for him to finish his shopping. Cables, adaptors, screws, a pair of pliers: all very professional, very specific, nothing at all like the cloudiness she moves in.

Outside, Píter walks next to her at a sportive pace, straight but flexible. His way of moving is so elegant, so different from the people around them, that Nat is proud to be walking alongside him: the kind of pride associated with legitimacy. When he points out the windows at the town hall, the spell is broken.

'Pretty, aren't they? I made them myself.'

The windows clash terribly with the building's exposed brick, but she is all praise: they suit it perfectly, she says. Píter looks at her appreciatively. Precisely, he says, that's what he seeks, that his work be appropriate to its context.

'Petacas isn't the prettiest place in the world, but, to the extent they can, people should work to make their surroundings more beautiful, don't you think?'

'So, you're a…' Nat doesn't know what you call a person who makes stained-glass windows.

'A glazier? Yes. Well, more than a glazier. You could say I'm a glass and colour artisan. Like, I don't just do windows.'

'Of course.' Nat smiles.

They have a beer in one of the bars on the square. The beer is ice-cold and goes down easy. Píter observes her closely – too closely, she thinks – but his eyes are sweet and that softens her discomfort. The conversation returns to the landlord – that cheeky bastard, he repeats – the tools and her barren plot. He insists on lending her what she needs. Just a matter of tidying the yard, clearing it for a table and some lawn chairs, then planting a few oleanders and yuccas, or some succulents suitable for the harsh climate. There's a huge nursery near Petacas, very cheap. If she wants, they can go together someday. Her plans for a vegetable garden appear to be scrapped. She doesn't even mention them again.

She devotes the next few days to the exterior part of the house. She rises early to avoid the heat, but even so, she sweats nonstop, and a grubby feeling stays with her all day. She scrubs the porch, scrapes, sands and stains the pergola's wood floor and beams, prunes the withered branches that run rampant, pulls weeds and removes bag after bag of rubbish – papers, dry leaves, metal, plastic, empty cans, more broken branches. The final result is basically a wide expanse of cracked dirt. If the house were hers, she thinks, she would put in a lawn, and maybe the oleanders Píter recommended – they would make a natural fence to shelter her from prying eyes. But that's dumb: the house isn't hers and she's not going to all that effort for nothing.

One morning, the gypsy from the village limits pokes her head in the gate and asks if Nat wants any flowerpots.

'I got tons,' she says.

She sells Nat a whole bunch for cheap. They're all old, but Nat isn't bothered by the chips on the glazed pots or the mildew on the terracotta ones. There are two huge urns as well, and once they're scrubbed clean, they strike her as lovely. Since they're quite heavy, the gypsy's husband helps her carry them home, accompanied by two of their three sons. Nat likes that family. They're rowdy and good-natured, they don't go around complaining all day like the shopgirl. The kids pet Sieso and, for the first time, she sees the dog wag his tail and turn in a circle with an instinct to play.

'Just take some cuttings when you're out and about and you'll have the garden ready in no time,' the husband says as he's leaving. 'You don't need the nursery.'

It's true. Nat picks plants from nearby houses, many of them empty, branches that poke through the fences around the properties and whose loss doesn't pose any problem to the owners. Nevertheless, Píter is annoyed when he finds out. Was that really necessary? Didn't he tell her there was a nursery nearby, a super cheap one? He could have given her a bunch of cuttings himself, whole plants even.

In fact, he gives her a hardy cactus already budding with fuchsia flowers. Nat reluctantly places it by the door. It's a marvellous specimen but its mere presence soaks up all the attention.

The change to the yard is undeniable. The cuttings take root and grow by the day. Roberta, the old woman in the small yellow cottage, comes over and offers her enthusiastic congratulations. Right away, Nat feels drawn to her. Why did the shopgirl call her a witch? If anything stands out about this woman, it's her sweetness. She must have been quite beautiful when she was young. Something of that beauty can be appreciated in the slender lines of her nose and mouth. Her eyes, though, are the most striking: dark, penetrating, warm. Her hair, fine and very white, spreads over her head like a light mist. The woman heaps praise on Nat's work. She tells her that since she arrived, it's all very different, and change – all change – is always good.

'Bad thing, stagnant water,' she winks.

Nat realizes the woman thinks she's bought the house. No one in their right mind would go to all this trouble for a rented hovel.

Even a crazy old lady can see that.

Words another person wrote before her: words chosen with care, selected from all the myriad possibilities and arranged in a singular fashion among the infinity of discarded combinations. These words impose themselves on her. If she wants to do her job well – and she does – she must take every one of those choices into account. But that line of thinking leads to exhaustion and paralysis. By dissecting the language so conscientiously, she strips it of meaning. Each word becomes an enemy, and the translation is a duel with a version of the text that both predates hers and is better. She's exasperated by her slow progress. Is it the heat, the solitude, the lack of confidence, the fear? Or is it simply – and maybe she should just admit it – her ineptitude, her clumsiness?

Things with Sieso aren't going as she'd hoped, either. The dog refuses to enter the house, coming and going as he pleases and ignoring any rules. He doesn't trust enclosed spaces – obviously the result of some trauma – but Nat can't understand why he still doesn't trust her after so many days in her company. She remembers how he played with the gypsies' kids and tries to pet him like they did – behind the ears, on his sides – but the dog behaves defensively and flees, visibly ill at ease.

As of late, a concerto of barks and howls kicks up around two or three o'clock in the morning, fanning out over several kilometres, as if all of La Escapa's dogs suddenly go mad. Nat wonders where they've come from, all these desperate dogs so full of aggression. They can't be the same animals she sees during the day, dozing or peaceably sniffing along the roads. And if they are, why the nocturnal transformation? Why, all at once, are the placid animals turning ferocious? And what if Sieso were to transform, enter the fray, get hurt? Afraid he might run off, she decides to tie him up. Perhaps her fear is overblown or misguided – that's what she tells herself in the mornings – but it's real and indisputable, even though he returns safely every night.

Her plans had not included tying Sieso to a stake, but she can't think of how else to control him. Whenever she saw a dog tied up before, it seemed cruel and she'd judged the owners harshly. Now she's doing the same thing, maybe for the same reasons. She promises herself that it is a temporary measure, that as soon as they establish a bond she'll leave him loose. Eventually, he'll end up sleeping in the house with her, to keep her company.

Píter, however, is not at all confident that Sieso will change. Every time he comes by to say hello to Nat, he glances at the animal and tells her not to bother: the dog, he assures her, is damaged. He urges her to give him back. The longer she waits, the harder it'll be. When will she decide to listen to him? Nat thinks how Píter, contrary to his mild image and even his nickname, is always looking for conflict, or at least when it comes to the landlord, setting her against him. And it's not just the issue of the fan – which he continually reminds her about – but the other problems around the house, and most of all, the dog. But if the landlord is such a bad person, what can they expect of Sieso, who lived with him and suffered who knows how many blows under his authority? Píter himself told her about the landlord's attitude towards his animals: use and then abandon them. If he's had Sieso since he was a pup, then it's what the dog has learned to expect.

Nat has a chance to change this, to turn the situation around, and just for this reason – because such a chance exists and is in her hands – she refuses to give up.

*

One morning, she puts him in the car to take him to the vet in Petacas. It's a quick decision, though it turns out to be more difficult than she imagined. Sieso resists getting in the car, he spins around and watches her sideways, suspicious. Finally, she manages to trick him with a piece of bacon as bait and push him inside once he's distracted. Whispering to keep him calm, she settles him on a blanket in the back seat. Sieso stays put, his legs stiff, a look of panic in his eyes. He whines softly but remains oddly immobile. During the drive, Nat keeps an eye on him in the rear-view mirror. His mouth is open, panting, head down, legs stiff, hackles up, and the bacon next to him goes untouched. The animal is frightened and she feels bad. But mostly, she feels the desire for it to be over as quickly as possible.

The veterinary clinic is on a dead-end street on the outskirts of Petacas. The place is empty. Not only are there no clients waiting, there's no waiting room. The vet, clearly a foreigner, receives her with irritation, as if she is intruding or interrupting him in the middle of another, much more important task. He asks the dog's name as he puts on a pair of plastic gloves. Sieso, she says, embarrassed. When he raises an eyebrow, she hurries to clarify that it's an affectionate name, only half-serious, and that she'll change it in the future.

'Animals don't understand irony,' he says. 'It's not good to be changing their names all the time.'

His diagnosis is conclusive. Sieso has ear mites and worms. His limp is the result of an improperly healed back leg, broken at some point, perhaps from being run over. He is, moreover, malnourished and unchipped. Otherwise, he says, washing his hands, he's a young dog, and undoubtedly deserves a better life.

'Where are his papers? Is he up to date on his vaccinations?'

'I don't know. They didn't give me any papers.'

The vet gives her a firm look.

'And you can't ask?'

'Yeah, I guess I could.'

Country people, he sighs. Nobody keeps track of these things. They're stupid and stubborn, and often cruel to the point of savagery. He was brought a greyhound the other day. The animal was torn to bits. Nothing he could do to save it. She simply cannot imagine how hard it is to work in a place like Petacas. Like running into a brick wall, he says, day after day. Nat listens wordlessly. Her problem now is an economic one. Chipping and deworming Sieso, plus buying good dog food, is going to cost a lot more than she'd bargained for. And still, she fears, there's the question of his shots. But even with the money she'll spend, the blow to her budget, the most unpleasant part of the process, the most costly, will be interacting with the landlord.

She puts the dog bowl in the kitchen so Sieso gets used to coming inside. Sometimes she manages to get him to stay a little longer, lying down beside her. It's never for long, he never seems entirely relaxed, but for Nat it's an accomplishment: having him there, close enough to touch. When she runs her palm over his back, she senses, under the fur, the agitation that dominates him still, a continuous pulsing flow. He jumps at the slightest noise or movement she makes and is off like a shot. Then she has to earn his trust all over again.

That's exactly what happens one morning, when she sees him tense, jump up, whine softly and go outside. A few seconds go by before Nat hears the Jeep come to a stop and footsteps on the gravel. It's the landlord, here to collect the rent. In cash, like they agreed. Like they agreed? Actually, she thinks angrily, she never agreed to anything. According to him, that's how they had to do it, if she wanted him give her a deal, that is. No bank transfers or deposits, he decreed. She didn't care either way, right? So now, because she'd tried to avoid an argument, she has him here inside the house, having rapped on the door and entered before Nat even had the chance to answer. Before she can even stand to greet him, he's looking around, evaluating the changes she's made, a half-smile playing on his lips. Such a skinny man, Nat thinks, so insignificant, yet he has the power to contaminate the house in just a few seconds. She takes out the rent money and hands it over to him in an envelope.

'You should let me know next time,' she says. 'I might not have been here.'

'Bah, don't worry about that. If you're not here one day, I'll come the next.'

He's also brought her the bills. Electricity and gas, which are monthly, and the water, to be paid every three months. The fact that she's only been there a month is irrelevant. The house was unoccupied before her, he says, so that bill, the water bill, is also her sole responsibility. The amount is outrageous. Just holding it, Nat's hand shakes.

'I told you already that the bath tap leaks. There's no way I've used this much.'

'What are you implying, that I should pay it?'

'I'm just saying that it wasn't me. It's the tap.'

'Not the tap's fault, girl. You're the one living here, aren't you? Well, you should have fixed it.'

She should have. Nat knows he is partly right, but she told him about it the first day and he did nothing, or rather, the solution he gave – fixing it himself – hadn't convinced her. She could have asked someone else for help. Píter, for instance, though he would have criticized her acquiescence. Or she could have simply called a plumber, like everyone else does. In any case, she'd been avoiding it. In the end, she got used to the sound of constant dripping. She turned her attention to other things. And now, here she is, literally left holding the problem.

Fine, she says. She'll pay the bill with next month's rent, if that's OK with him. The landlord grunts in the affirmative, not the least bit grateful for her concession. Without another word, he leaves in a huff.

Nat remembers only later that she never asked him about Sieso's shots, or the bed she wants him to take away. Doesn't matter, she tells herself quickly, it's not that important. The mere risk of prolonging their encounters is so upsetting that she prefers not to bring it up. She'll deal with it herself.

A plumber in Petacas agrees to come out to La Escapa the next day. That same morning, while still stretching in bed, Nat hears a noise in the bathroom. At first, she thinks Sieso has got himself loose and come in to look for her, but she dresses quickly, heart pounding, because those sounds are human not animal: footsteps, a bag dropping, a weak clearing of the throat, more footsteps on the tile. Nat shouts who's there, and she looks, terrified, into the bathroom. When she sees the landlord, she cries out again. It's fear at first, then indignation, and quickly fear again. What are you doing here, she shouts over and over, on the edge of hysteria.

The landlord laughs, tells her to calm down.

'Easy, girl, it's me, it's fine.'

He says he's come to fix the tap. Needed fixing, didn't it? Hadn't she said so? He thought she wasn't home, or that she was asleep, because he didn't hear anything when he pulled up.

'But you can't come in without warning me first! You shouldn't even have a key! Who told you that you can open the door whenever you want?'

He laughs again.

'Don't get lawyerly with me, girl. I already said I thought you weren't home.'

He explains that the house was on his way, so he decided to come by early; later he has some other errands in La Escapa, and this way he doesn't waste the morning. He tells her he'll be done in a few minutes anyway, it's a simple repair, anyone could have fixed that tap. Any man, he specifies, because she obviously wasn't capable of it. Nat can't stop shouting. She insists, her voice warped by nerves, that he doesn't have permission to come inside like this, that he must never do it again. The landlord purses his lips and hardens his stare.

32

'What, you think I'm going to rape you or something?'

He looks her up and down with scorn. Then he turns back to the bath and bends down, muttering and fiddling with his tools. He says – under his breath, although Nat hears him perfectly clearly – that he's sick of women. The more you give them, he says, the worse they think they have it. They're all crazy, they're neurotic. He continues working and complaining. Nat remains frozen in the doorway. Then she goes out onto the porch and waits there for him to finish, still shaking.

'Done,' he says a little while later. 'See? Wasn't a big deal.'

He leaves without saying goodbye.

Still seated on the porch floor, Nat tries to suppress her anxiety, restraining herself from calling the police, or Píter, or whomever, hugging her knees until the upheaval slowly gives way to a kind of calm. Even so, she forgets to notify the plumber, who turns up a few hours later and, despite not having anything to fix, charges her for the trip, nevertheless.

'I put off another client to come out here. This place is a pain to get to,' he apologizes.

Nat doesn't argue. It's true. This place is decidedly a pain.

She tells the vet Sieso hasn't had any shots. She'd rather lie and risk vaccinating him twice than have to speak to the landlord any longer than necessary. Her only option is to open her wallet and get it over with. The procedure, however, turns out to be slower than expected – slow and cruel. Just when the needle gets close, Sieso suddenly wrestles away. Nat is forced to pin him down while they muzzle him. She is startled by his viciousness, the curled lip and bared teeth. She fears this could be a step backwards. Sieso might never forget her betrayal, the way she conspired to hurt him.

She buys a harness, leash, plastic chew bones, a training whistle. It's going to be complicated, converting him into the calm, affectionate dog she needs, but she won't give up so easily. She is, in fact, taking active steps to achieve it. To have that evolution validated – though arduous, though minimal – gives her an intimate satisfaction, as if the dog's progress were also, indirectly, her own.

Still, his first afternoon out on the leash is exhausting. Sieso pulls and pants, almost strangling himself. Further along, he sits down in the middle of the road and refuses to budge. Nat drags him home having gone just a few metres. Back at her house, she sees Píter at her front door, holding a box. At the sight of her, he sets it down and stands, hands on hips.

'You are the most stubborn woman I have ever seen. What a foolish waste of your energy. What led you to put him on a leash? Dogs around here are never leashed.'

'I was just trying to teach him. The vet recommended it. In case I have to take him somewhere.'

'Where are you going to take him? That animal will give you trouble everywhere.'

Píter has brought over some vegetables he bought from the German. It's too much for just him, he explains, but the German, very astute, always sells them like this, in big batches, so they don't rot. There are radishes, cour-gettes, cucumbers, tomatoes, and some bulbs Nat can't identify. The German? she asks, still wounded by Píter's comments. She seems to recall a guy, not very tall, with a moustache and glasses, dark-haired, awkward and evasive, a guy she's passed on the road a few times, someone who's barely mumbled hello, never meeting her eye.

'Oh, thanks,' she says flatly. 'But I don't know what I'll do with all of it.'

Ratatouille? Chilled soup? Vegetable lasagna? There are a million recipes, Píter replies. Why doesn't she stop wasting her time with the dog and make something for the two of them? He can contribute as well – a main course. They could have dinner at his place and he could show her his studio. Tomorrow. How's that sound?

Nat accepts. He's invited her over too many times for her to keep putting it off. This time, though, it's different. This time, it's a proper invitation: dinner, drinks, chat, and all that implies. Nat isn't naïve, she knows the possible implications of Píter's invitation and although something inside of her still resists – a subtle but persistent aversion – she needs to surrender. Ever since the landlord invaded her house, her sleep has been restless; she thinks she hears the key turning in the lock, the door opening, footsteps approaching. She hasn't wanted to say anything to Píter because she knows what he'll say: she should report him to the police right away. He'll be unyielding and will condemn her passivity and indolence. She would rather say nothing, keep it all to herself. And yet, being so isolated isn't easy, it's good to have a friend, otherwise she'll go crazy. She wonders if all she wants is friendship, or protection, too, and if she would feel the same relief – or the same unease – if the invitation came from a woman. A female friend would fit the bill, surely, but wouldn't do much to alleviate her sense of defencelessness. Anyway, she tells herself, Píter is the one expressing his desire to protect her. She just has to let him do it. She isn't asking for anything he isn't already willing to give her.

Píter's house is on the west side of La Escapa, some ten minutes from Nat's. It's a pretty wooden building with a pitched roof, wide windows, and garden beds. The inside is cool and pleasant, and although the space is cluttered with objects, they all appear to occupy a particular place and have a precise function and purpose. When Nat enters the foyer, Píter's dog comes over to sniff at the pan in her hands.

'Stuffed courgettes,' she announces.

Píter laughs loudly, taking her arm and leading her to the kitchen. A similar pan sits on the counter, the same dish. They laugh, and the dog wags her tail and squeezes between them, looking for a pat. 'My Funny Valentine' is playing, maybe the Chet Baker version, but Nat doesn't ask – she never asks those sorts of questions. Píter pours her a glass of wine and brings her down to the basement to show off his workshop. There, too, everything is carefully organized, ready, even, for an exhibit: plans and sketches, glass fragments in baskets and boxes – classified by colour – tools hung on the wall, a broad table with a half-finished windowpane and soldering irons suspended from the ceiling. Nat would prefer to poke around on her own, but she listens politely to Píter's explanations as he details, step by step, the stained-glass fabrication process. A simple stained-glass window, he says, improves any house, no matter how humble. Of course, if they commission him for something more formal, or even institutional, he doesn't say no, but he prefers to work on a small scale, for regular people. Nat moves in to examine the windowpane on the table. Lambs and doves dance around a leafy tree. The multiple shades of green used for the leaves creates an impression of disorder, or imbalance. Nat isn't sure she likes it. Viewed up close, the composition strikes her as conventional and rather unrefined.

'I was inspired by Chagall for this series. By the windows he made for the University of Hadassah, in Jerusalem. You know them, I suppose, very famous...'

Nat doesn't have the faintest idea, but she nods anyway. She turns towards the wall, where other windows in the series lean, finished and ready to be installed. They're for a library, Peter explains, that's why he's put verses on them: by Pablo Neruda, Mario Benedetti and Wisława Szymborska. Nat reads them slowly before asking:

'And you can make a living with these?'

She immediately regrets the words. It's the kind of loaded question she hates to be asked. But Píter doesn't seem to be bothered; quite the opposite, in fact, he answers gladly, with pride.

'Of course.'

He spends very little on materials, he says. He uses mostly recycled glass. He actually finds the most valuable pieces in the trash. He is committed to austerity as a way of life. His mottos: throw nothing away; reuse everything you can; respect the Earth; minimal consumption, maximum depth.

'I have the feeling we're rather alike in that respect,' he says, and inside Nat, a swift twinge of concern alights.

During dinner, her suspicions abate. Maybe it's the wine, but it's also Píter's affability; he proves to be warm and even witty, making her laugh like she hasn't laughed in a long time. Nevertheless, she watches him from the corner of her eye as they clear the table and he opens another bottle of wine, finding that there's something about him she just doesn't like, something that makes her hang back. It's not his physical appearance. In fact, his body is solid and attractive. His brawn is undoubtedly erotic. And he undoubtedly goes out of his way to please: he's charming, a good neighbour, knows about books, music and movies, everything one supposes is interesting in certain circles – her circle. So? Nat wonders why he lives alone, why he hasn't mentioned a woman yet; she dismisses the possibility that he might be gay. Then she takes the glass he offers her and smiles. She forces herself to brush away her prejudices.

They go out into the yard to look at the stars. The night is clear and the Milky Way looms in the darkness, pure and immense. The tips of the blades of grass gleam, bathed in the nocturnal light, swaying, rocked by the wind. The dog sits off to the side, drooling: beautiful and majestic despite her age. They three observe the sky in silence. So pretty, Nat murmurs as, perplexingly, she simultaneously thinks: my period. When the moment comes, she can tell him she has her period.

He turns towards her, scrutinizes her with a different sort of smile.

'Can I ask you something?'

'Of course.'

'Why did you come to La Escapa?'

Nat stutters. Hadn't she already answered that? Why does everyone assume she has a hidden motive? She doesn't reply, but finishes the last of her wine. Píter apologizes. He doesn't mean to be nosy, he says. She doesn't have to tell him anything if she doesn't want to, but, if she does want to talk, he'd be delighted to hear her story.

'I left my job,' she says at last. 'I couldn't take any more.'

'What did you do?'

Nat pulls back. She doesn't want to go into detail. It was an office job, she says. Commercial translations, correspondence with foreign clients, stuff like that. Not badly paid work, but definitely a far cry from her interests. Píter lights a cigarette, squints with the first drag.

'Well, you're brave.'

'Why?'

'Because no one quits their job these days.'

Nat is irritated by the praise. She might have accepted it, under other circumstances, but now she's flooded with the desire to resist. Coming from Píter, the compliment sounds poisonous. Or maybe, she thinks, it's her perception, blurred by the alcohol, that makes her take it that way, twisted. No, she isn't brave, she retorts. She didn't go voluntarily. Not entirely. Does he want to know the real story? Píter leans in. Of course.

She stole something. She'd stolen, not out of necessity, but impulse. She never did comprehend why she did it. It wasn't for the thrill of the challenge, definitely not for greed. The object was just there and she simply took it. It belonged to one of the company's partners. To one of the partner's wives, to be precise; something valuable she left behind on a visit. Later, returning it got complicated. Even if she'd wanted to – and of course she had – it became impossible to restore order. She could return the stolen object, but not without consequences. She chose to keep quiet. They caught her in the end. They called her aside, they behaved with discretion. She had always been a good employee, qualified and responsible. They only asked why she had done it, and she couldn't answer. Well, they said, sometimes we don't know why we do what we do, right? Such benevolence made her suspicious. She couldn't believe that a simple warning was all she was going to get. Maybe someone had interceded on her behalf. Someone who, later, would make clear exactly what she owed them. Her absolution now had a price, and she wasn't sure she wanted to pay it. She didn't want to stay where, from then on, they would be looking over her shoulder, knowing she had something to hide. Where, if she kept working, it was thanks to her superiors' compassion and generosity, and under new terms of an unwritten contract.

Píter listens and nods, deeply concentrated on her story, but when Nat is finished, he simply repeats his initial compliment: she's brave, whatever she might say. She's been brave enough to break with everything. Someone else in her position would have kept her head down, he's sure of that. She shouldn't feel guilty. Sometimes, certain mistakes lead us to the right thing, a change of course or even a revelation. Isn't it a good thing that she's here now, starting a new life?

They toast and drink, but a shadow has fallen over them, polluting the air. A new life, Nat thinks, and immediately feels ashamed. Everything she has said is true, and yet, because of the way she told it – her choice of words, cadence, pauses and circumventions – it's topped with a halo of falseness that she finds repellent. Her need to justify herself, she thinks, is pathetic.

Seeing her wilt, Píter kindly changes the subject, asks her about her current work, about the translation. It's her first assignment, she explains. Her first literary translation, she clarifies. She's never done anything like it before. In fact, you might say she's being put to the test. The publishing house that offered her the job has faith in her abilities, but it represents a qualitative leap, that's for sure. Commercial translation is straightforward and this… well, what she's aiming for is the essence, the very heart of language.

Píter is interested in the book itself, less so in theoretical digressions. What's it about, he asks. Is it a novel? Essay? What? It's impossible to explain, Nat says. There's no unfolding plot that can be summed up in one or two sentences. They're theatrical pieces, very short, almost schematic, philosophical in tone. The author didn't write them in her mother tongue, but in the language of the country where she lived in exile, so the writing is very rudimentary, even flat. At first Nat thought this would be advantageous, but it's revealing itself to be a challenge. Now she finds herself obliged to decipher whether each unexpected or ambiguous word is an error based on a lack of knowledge of the language, or if it's an intended effect resulting from intense consideration. There's no way to know.

'And you can't ask the author?'

Nat shakes her head, irked. The woman died, which may be for the best. This way, she's spared the disappointment of witnessing the mess Nat is making of her book.

Píter smiles and looks back up at the sky. Nice profession, he says. Translation. Interesting and useful, he adds. Necessary. He sets aside his glass and, with a napkin, wipes his dog's mouth. The docile animal lets him do it, and in that placidity – and in Píter's manner – Nat sees great gentleness, but a kind of gentleness that is artificial, calculated. Sieso would never let anyone clean him like that. Maybe that's why Píter does it, to highlight the difference between the animals. When he's done, he fills Nat's glass again. Fuzzily, Nat thinks: he's getting me drunk. In the distance, a word takes shape – this – and then a complete sentence: this is how the charades begin.

Why doesn't Píter tell her anything about himself? Why does he just poke around, attempting to draw her out? Where does he get the authority to give her advice? Time for me to go, she announces, then realizes, upon standing, just how dizzy she is. She tries to dissimulate her wobbling as Píter takes her to the bathroom, where she stays a long time, until the alcohol's effects have somewhat dissipated.

It's very late when he offers to take her back to her house. He drops her off at her front door and asks her if she'll be all right. Nat nods and thanks him. Píter brushes her cheek softly, bids her goodnight – get some rest, he says – and that's it. Nat is surprised, disappointed even. Wasn't he going to kiss her, or at least try? He wasn't going to try to take her to bed? Isn't that the predictable thing, what's expected from a man? Why the Sam Cooke and the Miles Davis and so much wine, why the Milky Way? She had her excuse all ready for nothing. But then, would she have wanted anything different? No, definitely not, but she doesn't want this either, not the stumbling around in the entryway, the clumsy steps, the vertigo, and the total solitude of the shut-up house. Nat lurches towards her bed and then hears something, a sound approaching from the shadows. She feels her heart dropping to the floor, until she realizes that Sieso is licking her trembling hand. It is the first time the dog has shown her any sign of affection, a greeting. Excited, she crouches, cries, talks to him.

'You scared me!'

She hugs him. His coarse fur gets in her nose and eyes, but still she hugs him, so tight that eventually Sieso wriggles away with a growl.

Her relationship with Píter becomes closer after that night. Having revealed certain things to him, Nat is at a disadvantage, but this asymmetry doesn't worry her: she hasn't told him everything – not even close. His attitude hasn't changed following her confidences. If anything, he is even more affable, more affectionate. They text each other throughout the day and Nat often visits him at home; she no longer needs an invitation and goes over whenever she feels like it or is bored. Following her intuition, she steers clear of information she believes would be inconvenient to share. She doesn't tell him, for instance, about Sieso's gradual progress or her fear of the landlord. What for? Píter's tendency to insert himself into everything, his patronizing tone – the supposed voice of experience, because he's a man, because he's older, because he's been in La Escapa longer, because he's friends with all the people whose names Nat barely knows – doesn't seem serious enough to impede their friendship.

What became obvious during the dinner – that there is no sexual attraction between them – contributes, paradoxically, to their closeness. And yet, Píter's disinterest sets off alarm bells for Nat: a sign that she is starting to lose a power that, until now, she had unconsciously possessed. Like money, she says to herself, erotic capital also imperceptibly erodes over time, we only become aware of it when it's gone, and she scrutinizes herself in the mirror with merciless eyes, evaluating the parts of her body or face where the flaw might reside. True, she has let herself go since she arrived in La Escapa. Her hair is messy and coarse, the work clothes do nothing for her, and the hours spent in the sun, instead of bronzing her skin, have left it red and parched. But there must be something else. Something to do with age, or the pressing weight of time, not its passing.

She'd rather not think about it. As with so many other things, she sets the idea aside, quarantined.

Sometimes she has the sense that the landlord has used his key again, to enter the house in her absence. There is no demonstrable proof, nothing out of place, no evidence of his presence, but the mere possibility – a real possibility, as she has seen – is weighty enough to distress her. She forces herself to be rational. She must dispel her suspicions and not obsess. Yet all it takes is closing her eyes and relaxing her consciousness for the landlord's spectre to waltz in, in the shape of a nightmare.

She has a recurring dream in which she discovers a window beside her bed. It's a new window that appears overnight. The roller shutters are half closed and a pair of white curtains partially obscure the view outside. Through the window, or what little can be seen through it, she perceives an unfamiliar but perfectly realistic landscape. The scene is not always the same: sometimes there are snow-capped mountains under a sooty sky, or a rough sea, or blocks of very tall buildings on the outskirts of a city, with all their lights on. When, fascinated, she tries to sit up to get a better look, she realizes she is tied to the headboard – or the bed frame or legs – with ribbons knotted at her wrists. They don't seem like much, the ribbons, but she is completely immobilized by them. Nat doesn't know who has tied her up, nor when. She observes the knots pressing on her veins, the chafing on her skin, her fingers that tingle with the lack of circulation. Fear takes hold. At that moment, she hears the front door opening and a man coming inside with slow, shuffling footsteps he makes no effort to conceal. Nat wonders where Sieso could be, why he hasn't barked to warn her. Never leaving the bed, she can somehow see the man making his way through every room in the house – a much bigger house than she'd thought, with a multitude of rooms she didn't know were there: storage closets, attics, small rooms inside other rooms. She sees the man, his back, his bare, staunch neck, and watches as he enters every space, contaminating them with his very presence. But she cannot see his face. The man comes to the side of her bed. Something in her throat goes spongy, muffling her scream. Nat is suffocating.

She wakes up sweaty, limbs heavy and gums parched. The night sounds mix with her still-confused senses: a horse's nervous whinny, the hoot of a brown owl, dense cricket song, and the dogs, always the dogs, their over-lapping barks.

But worse are the noises she discovers, even seeks, inside the house. Every day, every night, dreaming or not. Creaks and squeals, air whistling through the shutters, the fan's hum, Sieso's toenails click-clacking on the old wooden porch as he paces around the stake. None of the noises are associated with the landlord, but her guard is up. When he comes with the second month's bills, he knocks on the front door. Nat's relief is so great that she pays without complaint. This is better, she tells herself. Don't ask for anything, finish up quickly, then be free of his face until the following month.

After so many days and so many walks, she knows all the trails like the back of her hand, all the houses and who lives in them, but she can't shake the sense that something is slipping away from her, that there are things she can't see or understand. El Glauco's hulking form is omnipres-ent; no matter where she looks, there it is. Even with her back turned, it stalks her. I can't escape that mountain, she says to Píter. It's like I'm always being watched. But try to imagine La Escapa without El Glauco, he says: nothing but flatlands, no personality, just the same as everywhere else. She's uncomfortable with difference, he says solemnly, and she realizes they're talking about separate things, like they almost always do.

She is keenly drawn to one abandoned house. Someone has written *god's punishment* and also *shame* in big red letters on its crumbling walls. Píter tells her that a couple used to live there, a long time ago now, a brother and sister who, according to the rumours, had an incestuous relationship. They fled to La Escapa from another village and stayed a few years, reclusive and in a notable state of poverty, because no one would give them work, avoiding the insults and even attacks as best they could. Once, Píter says, somebody threw rocks through their windows and, another time, set fire to their shed. The man, who must have been about fifty, died from a sudden heart attack; a few days later, his sister, who was younger and appeared to be mentally disabled, abandoned the house, leaving it exactly as it was. Almost immediately, the same people who had disavowed them with such disgust showed up to make off with anything useful. Everything else they maliciously destroyed in a big bonfire. The graffiti was added later.

But all of that happened ages ago, Píter rushes to add. It's a kind of urban legend. He didn't even live here back then, he's just recounting what he was told. She shouldn't get a bad impression of La Escapa, things have changed a lot since then, people are increasingly more tolerant, more civilized. If that were true, Nat thinks, someone would have bothered to scrub the graffiti off. The words, still there, displayed for all to see, strike her as some kind of reminder. A warning, even.

She can spend whole days roaming and, except for the construction crews, only run into the gypsy husband collecting scrap metal or running errands, Joaquín – Roberta's husband – or the German, who drives his van back and forth to Petacas, presumably to sell the vegetables from his garden. If it weren't for Píter, she might not speak to anyone for days. Now that she's not a novelty, not even the shopgirl takes an interest in her. She simply rings up Nat's shopping, her eyes glued to the TV mounted in the corner. Her boredom gives off a whiff of despair. Nat watches her crack her knuckles, lost in thought, humming under her breath. Her still-adolescent face contains the template for how she will be when she's fifty or sixty, when she's plagued by the same migraines as her mother. Nat would like to be kind to her, but can't think of anything to say.

Sometimes she goes with Píter to Gordo's bar, a warehouse with an asbestos ceiling lit by a single bulb emanating blue-tinged light. They drink bottles of beer with the men who stop in: farmers and bricklayers mostly, people who discuss matters about which Nat has nothing to add. Píter chats with them easily, though she has the impression that he's acting, getting down on their level. Sometimes Gordo charges extra, sometimes he doesn't charge at all, and no one's allowed to argue. There's always a hint of aggression, of provocation, in the way he jokes with his customers but they all laugh it off. Nat does, too. She would never go to that place alone, but with Píter it's different.

Weekends are livelier. The house next to Nat's, nick-named The Cottage – so reads the colourful sign on the gate – is occupied by a young couple with two small children, a boy and a girl, who spend the day out in the yard, shouting back and forth as if that were the most natural and only way to communicate. The woman, slim and chatty, seems welcoming, although she looks at Nat sceptically, maybe because she doesn't quite get what she's doing there alone, in that dreary, ill-equipped house, with that unfriendly dog. Píter, a long-time friend of the couple, made their upstairs windows, which lend the interior a warm quality, a reddish or orange-tinged hue, depending on the angle of the sunlight. The neighbour tells Nat that she inherited The Cottage unexpectedly from a great-aunt. At first, they tried to sell it, but they had no luck: nobody wanted to buy such a dark, dingy place. Instead, she says with a sigh of resignation, they capitalized on its potential, did some renovations so the kids could at least enjoy life outdoors. Her husband, the more enthusiastic of the two, mows the lawn with exacting regularity and amuses himself building playhouses and swing sets for their kids.

Nat is grateful when Monday comes and she can relax again.

One Sunday, the neighbours organize a barbecue and invite lots of people, almost all of them city friends who come out to La Escapa expressly for the party. Nat and Píter are also invited. Nat wants to go, but once there she shyly keeps to herself, drinking and observing the others from a corner. She's not entirely sure why many of the guests walk around the yard in their bathing suits. It makes no sense, she thinks, since they don't have a pool, not even an inflatable one, just a garden hose they use to cool off or play with, like little kids. The scene is almost obscene: an immodest parade of imperfect bodies, half-naked and wet. They talk seamlessly about gastronomy and politics, sometimes about both topics at once. They pretend to be well informed, which makes Nat withdraw even further. Some come over to chat, to ask about her life. They're curious about her presence in La Escapa, which has no obvious justification. Others think she's Píter's new girlfriend and behave accordingly, referring to them as you guys, which she doesn't bother to correct. All seem to find the idea of a retreat to the countryside, varnished with a romantic sheen, quite appealing. Nat wishes she could tell them that she's only there because it was the cheapest place she could find.

Later, she discovers the neighbour woman's eyes fixed on her from across the yard.

'I'm afraid she's jealous,' Píter says confidentially. 'Her husband won't stop talking about you. Haven't you noticed?'

She has. The husband was the one who took it upon himself to introduce her to their friends – pride in his voice when he said her name – the one who insisted on emphasizing particular details – that she's worked hard to fix up the house, that she's rescued a street dog, that she's a translator – the one who made sure she always had a drink. A perfect host, but at the expense of his other guests.

So all is not lost, Nat thinks. Her gratification, however, includes a measure of mockery. This is how it always is, and she can't help but see it from the outside. A male on the hunt for new prey to fall at his feet: his penetrating gaze, so wilfully seductive, and then his humped back and flat feet, the ridiculous bald spot when he turns around. She is amused. How absurd some men are.

On another day, Píter encourages her to participate in a residents' meeting; not everyone from La Escapa will be there, but she should go, her opinion matters. What kind of meeting? Nat asks cautiously. She is irritated by the obligation couched in Píter's suggestion, and she isn't entirely sure about her role as a resident; she considers herself a newcomer, without voice or vote. La Escapa is a godforsaken parish, Píter explains, despite having a village mayor, who is – just imagine – the shop owner, a man who enjoys his power more than he lets on. Be that as it may, his authority isn't of much use: the rest of them must also step up and demand that the Petacas town hall – La Escapa's genuine administrative oversight – do something. Oddly enough, the people behind the meeting are the owners of The Cottage, Píter himself, and a few others from the new batch – that's his expression, the new batch. People who want to improve things. But what things, Nat asks, what things.

'You don't look very enthused.'

'It's not that. I just don't know what good I'd do at the meeting. I'm just a renter, my landlord should be there.'

'Your landlord doesn't care about the issues. You know what he's like.'

SARA MESA

She does. And she knows that Píter is partly right, even though that's hard for her to admit. He mentions the need to improve refuse collection, the poor lighting on the roads, which are treacherous by night, and the danger posed to car tires by all those potholes and dips.

'Your tires too, right?'

She nods: hers too. Ultimately, she agrees to go.

They hold the meeting in the shop. On arrival, Nat is surprised to see that they almost don't fit, although, as Píter had predicted, not all residents are in attendance. The gypsy family, for instance, aren't present, and Nat senses that for some they represent as big a problem as the potholes. Neither is Gordo, who apparently doesn't get along with the shop owner – they want to kill each other, Píter whispers. Old Joaquín has come with Roberta, possibly because he doesn't have anybody to stay with her. The old woman isn't having her best day. Halfway through the meeting, she begins to speak incoherently in a brittle voice, and even though her speech is perfectly articulate, the words she uses are seemingly unconnected: complicated words with limited meanings like manatee, wetland, turbidity and gland. Nat recalls that those exact words appeared in a film that aired on TV at midday. It was a tremendously boring documentary about the Antilles, which must have caught the old woman's attention and disorientated her, because her manner of speaking contains a desperate, questioning timbre: what does all of this mean, she seems to say, why are they arguing about things she doesn't understand – things like pavements, streetlights, rubbish bins – as if parading through her head are oceanic images and disjointed words.

Joaquín simply waits while his wife speaks, showing no hint of embarrassment, confident that the others will do the same – wait, resigned and courteous – but Nat senses the impatience, the glances, the throat-clearings. Píter smiles condescendingly, the couple from The Cottage whisper between themselves, the shop owner makes a face. Only the German remains unperturbed as he leans against some boxes of tin cans, head down, looking at his boots, which he slowly taps from side to side. Nat focuses on him. Why has he come to the meeting, as solitary and independent as he seems to be? Nat doesn't know why they call him that, the German, since he isn't German and doesn't look how one assumes a German would look, based on the stereotype, of course, of a blond, strong, Teutonic figure. No, the man is small, with dark, thinning hair and a receding hairline. His nose is broad and ugly, his moustache droops, and the glasses he wears for nearsightedness don't make him look sophisticated, but utterly local instead. The German must be a nickname, just like Píter is the hippie and Roberta the witch. People usually go by nicknames in small villages, don't they? Nat wonders if they've given her one, too. She isn't sure she wants to know.

She discovers a small snake coiled up in the woodpile. It's a snub-nosed adder, with an insolent snout and a scowling, concentrated expression. Nat jumps back. As a girl, she heard that their venom is fatal, that it can kill a man in half an hour. She must get rid of it quickly, but she is afraid it will slither towards her if she tries to kill it. Besides, how would she do it? The thought of smashing it with a stick is repellent. She goes in search of aid. It takes a while to find someone willing to lend her a hand. Píter is in Petacas and the workmen tell her they have a lot of stuff to get done. One of them promises to come by when they finish their project, but Nat can't wait. Finally, she manages to get the gypsy husband. Not only does he not object, but he comes quickly and readily, rolling up his sleeves. The adder hasn't moved. Sluggish under the sun beating down on the logs, the reptile remains still but expectant, as if it anticipated the danger, watching out of the corner of its golden eye, its terrifying, vertical pupil. The gypsy uses a rock to smash it to death. Blood glistens on its wrecked scales and the sight makes Nat feel sick. Relief, however, outweighs her disgust. She opens her wallet, looking for something to give the gypsy, but he holds up his hand, reassuring and perhaps a little offended.

'Oh knock it off. I've killed plenty of these things... if they paid me every time, I'd have an Audi and a three-storey house by now.'

Later, Píter will say that she shouldn't have killed it. Snub-nosed adders aren't poisonous, that's nothing but an old wives' tale. Prejudices and unsubstantiated fears, that's the way of things, he says, shaking his head sadly. Does she really think that a snake barely more than half a metre long would waste its venom, its rare, precious venom, on a human? No, a viper like that never attacks, not unless someone antagonizes it the way they did.

'What should I have done then?' Nat asks.

'Nothing. Leave it alone. Or pick it up carefully and move it somewhere else. They were here before us, weren't they?'

Nat concedes that he's right – what choice does she have – but she thinks: even a common adder has pre-emptive rights over her land. No matter how much time passes, she will always be an interloper.

One night, the wind changes direction and the temperature drops. Nat is reading on the porch; first she gets a cardigan, then decides to go inside, still too chilly. Hot, fat raindrops promptly begin to fall and within a couple of minutes the downpour begins, raising a new, encouraging scent from the wet earth. Nat is as happy as a child. She feels like she has made it to the end of a phase, the first and most challenging, and that the rain marks the start of a new and more promising one. But her joy is short-lived: it lasts as long as it takes for the leaks and a swiftly widening puddle to appear. Nat runs for some buckets and when she returns, her hair and clothes soaked through, mud has already started to form inside the house. Incredible, she thinks. What does one do in these situations? And how hadn't she noticed before? Hadn't she seen the yellow stains on the ceiling a thousand times? What did she think they were? She spends half the night emptying buckets and putting them back, until the storm wanes and she can lie down to rest. She sleeps in intervals, afraid the rain will start up again, knowing that this time she'll have no choice but to call the landlord. But the sky is radiant in the morning, without a trace of cloud. Can she put the call off? At least until the next time he comes with the bills? With any luck, it won't rain again before then; better to wait, not to wake the dragon too soon. She knows she's making excuses to avoid the problem, but, she tells herself, they aren't really excuses, they're actual facts: the sky doesn't threaten more rain, it was just a passing August rainstorm, nothing to worry about for now.

Her forecast is correct: no drops fall over the coming days. She almost manages to forget the issue, but not quite. Whenever she looks up, she is confronted by the stains, which look like limescale or urine and gross her out. When the month ends and the landlord shows up in his grubby coverall, Nat shows him the stains. He squints to inspect them. She tells him what happened the night of the downpour, about the puddles and buckets. She explains that this is why the wood floor is rotting. This is irrefutable proof, she thinks. He cannot deny the evidence.

'Well, girl, it doesn't rain like that every day.'

'Not every day, no. But it could happen again. I mean, it'll definitely rain this autumn, right? Maybe not as hard, but the leaks are there and...' She falters. 'The floor is getting ruined...'

The landlord looks at her breasts as she speaks. He's doing it on purpose, Nat thinks. To destabilize her, she thinks. Humiliate her. Lip curling, he says the rotting floor isn't her problem. Not her house, is it? She's just a renter, he repeats, a renter who has done nothing but complain ever since she arrived.

'What do you want me to do? You think the shitty rent you pay is enough for me get bogged down in a bunch home improvements?'

Nat, furious, is incapable of expressing her anger. She wants to be forceful. Instead, she just sounds hesitant and scared.

'So the next time it pours, I'm just supposed to put out buckets?'

'Exactly!'

He points a finger at her and she weakens. Her throat burns and she feels a scorching sensation that reaches her eyeballs. Is she going to cry? She cannot let that happen. She must contain the urge, no matter what.

'I think… all of this just isn't… I don't think this is normal.'

'No? Don't think it's normal, do you? And just what do you think is normal, girl? To come out to the middle of the country and expect a cushy city life?'

He begins to speak in plural then, throwing his arms about, pacing in circles.

'You women are all the same. You think this is all starry skies at night and little lambs baaing in the morning. Then you're on about the mosquitoes, the rain, the weeds. Look, I already brought the price way down. Did I bring it down or not? Or don't you remember now? When you've had a problem, haven't I fixed it? Didn't I fix the tap? Oh, you thought that was horrible, too. Can't understand you women. Look, I got a lot more important things to do. Give me my money and get off my back.'

Nat pays him and he leaves, slamming the door behind him. She cries then, full of rage because she cannot understand what it is about the landlord that so terrifies her. A rude, small-minded man with no actual power over her. Is he not clearly inferior? Uneducated, dirty and poor, what damage can he do? Why does he have such an effect on her? She cries and, at the same time, tries to convince herself that maybe there won't be more leaks, maybe putting out a few buckets when it rains is fine, maybe that was an unusual storm, maybe it's not really that big of a deal, maybe she can hold out for a few months. It isn't her house, after all, she'll end up moving out sooner or later. In the meantime, it's better to be chill, not stress, not let herself get upset. This is how she will defeat him, how she will stay on top.

But the stains continue to speak for themselves. This time, it's the German who sees them when he comes around, offering her a crate of vegetables. He sets the box down in the entryway and he stops at the ruined floorboards. He looks up and examines the ceiling.

'You've got leaks.'

He has an odd way of speaking, knocking his syllables together, like he's in a rush or being abrupt. Without meeting her eye, he asks for a chair and climbs up for a closer look. Nat notices his boots – sturdy and worn, the same pair he had on at the meeting – as he explains the cause of the problem.

'Looks like it's been like this a long time. There are probably a decent number of broken tiles up there. You'd need to check and see if they can be fixed, but I doubt it. When the leaks are superficial, you can just cover the tiles with bitumen or lime, but I'm afraid this is more complicated. What'd your landlord say?'

'That it only leaks when there's heavy rain. That it's not his problem. And that he's not going to do anything.'

The German gets down from the chair, shakes his head.

'As soon as it rains again, even just a sprinkle, this will all flood again. I could fix it for you.'

Nat appreciates that he doesn't comment on the land-lord's stance. She likes that he doesn't judge her, that he doesn't deem the situation as fair or unfair, doesn't urge her to argue or defend her position. The German sticks to the facts and sees the situation head-on, without his own interpretation. This attitude is precisely what gives her licence to vent and complain.

'It's ridiculous that I have to fix it. He should do it, right? It's his house.'

'Yeah. His house, but your problem. I can help you, seriously. I know how to fix it.'

To prove this, he describes the process in detail: first, they need to evaluate how far the damage goes; then, look for similar tiles and retile the affected area. Finally, channel the runoff with either grating or gutters so it doesn't happen again – they'd see about that later. But they're not friends, Nat thinks. She'll have to pay him. And how much could something like that cost? She doesn't have much money, but also won't accept any favours. She doesn't distrust him, but she doesn't want to owe him anything.

'I don't know if I can afford it,' she says.

The German is silent. She suspects he is about to offer to do it for free. But after a few seconds, he says he under-stands. He can't estimate how much it will cost before getting started. He doesn't want to fix one problem and cause another. He shrugs and, for the first time, looks at her. There's no disappointment in his eyes, or resignation, just a trace of timidity and kindness, maybe a bit of embar-rassment. It could be that he's short on cash as well, and saw a chance to earn a little extra income. He seems honest to Nat, but uncouth. All she can do is cross her fingers in the hope that it doesn't rain and buy bigger buckets just in case. She pays for the vegetables, says thanks, and walks him outside.

What happens just two hours later will be meticulously remembered by Nat afterwards, with a need to secure the details in place so as not to forget any of it, to prevent memory from perverting, adulterating or disguising it.

In her recollection, a word – droit – will echo, as well as a phrase – le droit de sauver – from a dialogue she was translating when it happened. *You do not have the right to save whomever you want,* one of the characters protests, and the other replies: *It is not a right, it is a duty!*

Nat is writing those very words when she hears someone call her name. She stands and goes outside and it's him, the German, waiting outside the gate, even though it has stood open since he left. She notices that he's changed his clothes: the faded grey trousers for a different pair, clean and blue, the black T-shirt advertising a mechanic's shop for a beige shirt, so threadbare it's almost see-through. He doesn't smile, but he isn't serious either. Rather, he gives off the impression that he's focused on something – something he's about to do or say and which doesn't seem directly related to Nat. It occurs to her that he might have forgotten something, or maybe she paid him the wrong amount for the vegetables, or maybe he's going to offer to fix the leaks for free after all, like she'd suspected. His glance at the roof tiles confirms that it's the third option. Predictable, she thinks, although she could have never foreseen what came next.

'I don't want you to get mad,' he says.

He stops at that, studying the roof, squinting in the sun-light. Sieso approaches him slowly, sniffs his trouser legs.

'Mad? Why would I get mad?'

It takes him a while to find the words, but this delay doesn't seem to suggest any discomfort with the message, but rather an uncertainty about the use of language itself. Waiting for him to speak, Nat is intrigued, albeit slightly indifferent, as if what he was about to say – or propose, since it's obviously a proposal – didn't concern her.

'I guess you have the right to get mad. It's a risk I'll take.'

It's not a right, it's a duty! Nat thinks, but she smiles, encouraging him to speak.

'Come on, just say it, it's fine.'

He says it. He says he's been alone for a long time. A long time without a woman, he specifies. Living in La Escapa doesn't help. Neither does having a personality like his, cut off and reserved – although he doesn't use those adjectives: he says, simply, a personality like mine. It's not like he's unhappy. He's not sad or depressed, that isn't it. But the fact is, men have certain needs. At this his voice cracks a bit, though he steadies it right away. He's not that young any more, he continues, some ten or twelve years older than she is – he looks her over, evaluating her. He doesn't feel old, but neither does he have the energy to pick women up. He smiles, embarrassed, and Nat senses that it isn't because of what he means, but the expression pick up – so euphemistic and antiquated, out of place. To meet women, he corrects himself. His smile fades. He doesn't want to resort to prostitutes: the ones in Petacas

61

are awful, he says, all of that completely turns him off. She nods mechanically.

It's very simple, really, the German continues. Or it should be. Even though men and women rarely think about it that way. No one dares to speak openly. What's normal – or common – is to have ulterior motives. He thinks that maybe with her, he can cut right to the chase. It's just an intuition he has, but maybe she'll misinterpret him and get offended, or she could interpret him correctly and still be offended. He doesn't know her well enough to anticipate how she will react; the only way to know is to just throw it out there. He waits a few seconds, searching her face.

'I can fix your roof, if you let me inside you for a little while.'

Nat will repeat these words to herself later, over and over until she is afraid that she's made them up. He doesn't say if you let me sleep with you. He certainly doesn't use any other expression, more or less offensive, with a similar meaning. If you let me, he says. A strange way to put it, and not the result of a deficient command of the language – he's not German, after all! Let him inside, she repeats to herself. A little while, he said. A little while. Nat blinks. She needs to hear more, or perhaps to hear it more times in order to understand it. But his attitude – the loose arms, legs apart, the humble, evasive eyes – seems to indicate that he has finished speaking and is now, quite simply, awaiting a response.

'And how would that be, exactly?'

The German looks at her for a moment and tries to smile, but the expression is closer to a wince. Of relief? Of satisfaction, because she isn't angry? Nat wouldn't possibly know how interpret it. Just once, he specifies. A little while, he repeats. The minimum, he says next.

'I won't pester you. I don't want to be a bother. You're not a prostitute, I don't want you to think that I take you for one. It's just—' He hesitates. 'I'd like to be inside you for a little while. Simple as that. You lie down and I'll be done fast. That's all. It's been a long time since I was with a woman. My body needs it. I thought I could ask you.'

Afterwards, Nat will remember these words, too. The coolness of his statements, so short and direct. His concision. He could have said what people usually say in those situations. He could have said, for example, that he liked Nat, that he was attracted to her, that he was risking such a request because he could hardly resist her pull. But those last words – I thought I could ask you – mean nothing. He isn't asking Nat because he likes her, but because he thought he could ask her. So, who can he not ask? Who doesn't he ask because he believes he cannot?

Subtle but instinctive, Nat allows herself to operate from irritation, as well as impatience. The reaction lasts only an instant, but it is decisive in her refusal, which springs curt and direct from her mouth, catching her almost by surprise.

'Thanks, but no.'

OK, he says, and calmly makes to leave. He doesn't press, but neither does he apologize. Nat says goodbye as though, in effect, nothing strange had occurred.

But back at her desk, she is unable to resume her work.

It will be several days before she can.

It rains. Not a heavy rain, but gentle and steady with no peaks or troughs. It starts at midnight. Nat makes Sieso come inside, sets out the buckets, and stays alert, emptying them before they overflow. The floorboards give off a damp, sticky heat that makes her sleepy. She sinks sluggishly into an elaborate dream, a dream that picks back up after each interruption, never breaking off completely. In this dream, Sieso has run off and she chases after him, but she's barefoot and the only shoes on hand are a pair of sturdy leather boots, like the German's. They are not the most appropriate footwear; the boots are so heavy she can hardly lift her feet off the ground, she can barely move. No matter how desperate she is, how much she hurries, she's already lost sight of the dog and can only hear his increasingly weak whines. When she wakes, she realizes that Sieso's whining is real, and his sounds have infiltrated her dreams. But the boots? Were they real? Real or not, she thinks, they are not the solution to her problem.

The rain, and the revelation, disappear with the dawn. Nat observes the sky. Dense black storm clouds amass over El Glauco; it won't be long before it rains again. Now, however, in the plain light of day, she's calm. The leaks, she thinks, aren't such a big deal. She just has to replace the buckets when required; surely, there are people who live in worse conditions and still get on with life, uncomplaining. The German's offer, his voice – his voice making the offer – still echoes in her head, but she isn't worried. The German is in her memory just like he was on her doorstep a few days ago, speaking with surprising serenity. She will take it the same way. Dispassionately.

The bad weather will continue throughout the week, although it won't ever become unmanageable. It rains and stops, rains and stops, a tranquil rhythm, good for the crops. Even so, the leaks persist because there's no time for the roof to dry out between downpours. Nat spends hours and hours minding the buckets. She can barely leave the house except to buy the bare necessities. The days pass and her fatigue builds. She watches the sky with discouragement. A growing angst coalesces within her.

One midday, when the rain lets up and a few breaks in the clouds are visible on the horizon, she leaves the house to stretch her legs. Sieso follows her to the gate, where he stands stock-still despite her persistent calls.

'Stay there, then,' she snaps. 'Your choice.'

The dog watches her walk away down the road. Though the air has cooled, Nat is dressed for summer in a simple pair of shorts and a cotton T-shirt. She crosses her arms to protect herself from the chill and presses onward into the headwind. She passes Píter's house with barely a glance in its direction. She strides ahead, almost mechanically, though she'd never be so naïve as to deny that she knows perfectly well where she's going. She does know, in effect, but not why or what for, just like she doesn't know the source of her anger, or more than anger, her vexation.

A fleeting thought enters her mind, so quick there isn't time to catch and understand it. Something about primitive exchanges. Bartering as a basic social interaction. Why not. There's something beautiful there. Something essential and human.

The house she stops at looks a lot like hers. Unassuming, single-storey, low windows. The main difference is that the yard is around the back, not out the front, and so she has to stand directly at the door, which is ajar. She clears her throat and gives a timid knock. She realizes suddenly that she doesn't know the German's real name. She pokes her head inside, says anybody home, but it sounds more like a statement than a question. Her voice, in fact, doesn't sound like her own, it sounds fake, like she is reading a part in a play. Anybody home, she repeats. Since there is no answer, she steps inside. The house smells like damp wood and toast. There are a few pieces of furniture, clothes hung on a foldable drying rack, a television set, small and obsolete, on a shelf. A tiger cat watches her from a tabletop, completely motionless. Nat walks past the cat, crosses the house, and exits through the back door leading to the garden. The German is squatting next to some furrows in the dirt. He turns and looks at her, unsurprised, as if her arrival had only been a matter of time. He wipes his forehead on a forearm.

'You came.'

He approaches her, hesitant. Nat observes him, muddy, sweaty and ungainly, with his glasses askance, and recalls what he said days before – it's been a long time since I was with a woman – and she understands, right then and there, how crucial that sentence is to his offer, and the dimension Nat herself invests in those words. What is she about to do? Have charity sex?

'Did you change your mind?' he asks. 'The rain make you change your mind?'

Nat nods.

'You want it now? Here?'

Instinctively, she nods again. Suddenly, the question seems impertinent, almost absurd, but he's already dropping his tools, brushing off his hands.

'Give me a few minutes. I'm going to shower.'

He smiles at her as he goes inside: a tight smile, embarrassed, maybe, although too bright and quick. She stays outside, looking at the garden. Another pair of skittish cats, skinnier than the one inside, pass her on their way to the shed at the back, where sacks, logs and tools are stored. The earth exhales a strong smell of manure, or rubbish. Nat studies the sky, the clouds crowding in the distance. The smell, the wind on her skin, the mix of green and brown hues, the leaves and dirt, the bitter taste of her saliva, her nerves: everything that anchors her to that moment is experienced through her senses, and yet, the unreality is overwhelming; the conceptual eclipses the material, as if instead of being on the edge of a new lived experience, she is an actor on set, participating in a great big lie. The German doesn't take long. He comes outside for her with wet hair combed back. He points to the rotting pepper plants.

'What's good for some plants ruins others.'

She realizes he is just talking to lower the tension. His commentary, however, only makes it worse. A crease of anger inches towards her mouth. She needs it to be over as soon as possible. He seems to notice and so he leads her inside, where, after gently taking her arm, he points to a darkened bedroom. His voice softens as he explains that it's better this way, in the dark. He doesn't want her to be uncomfortable, he says. He doesn't want her to feel upset or offended, he repeats.

'We'll finish quickly.'

When her eyes adjust to the dark, Nat sees a small, unmade bed. He asks her to lie down, please, on her back. She can take off all her clothes or just what's necessary, whatever she prefers. Nat lies on the bed and strips from the waist down, while the German turns away, as if he'd rather not watch. The sheets are slightly damp but clean, as if he had put them on before they were completely dry. Still facing away, he explains what they will do. Nat finds a kind of professional detachment in his words. Not indifference, but rather a reminder that their encounter constitutes a commercial transaction. And yet, beneath his voice there's a tremble of uncertainty, an inability to entirely contain his unease. Nat feels a tenuous tenderness then, something ephemeral that instantly disappears. She thinks: here is a man I would never be attracted to. This is how it must be, like this, in the shadows: a man attempting to hide his nervousness as he removes his shirt and pants; a woman waiting, ready to surrender, not really knowing what purpose that surrender serves.

That's how she sees it then: as a surrender, a handing over. Something she cedes to him in exchange for something else.

Everything unfolds according to plan. He is already very aroused when he climbs on top of her. First on his knees, gauging the space between her legs, his head bent, not meeting her eyes. Nat sees the shape of his penis, observing it with curiosity as he opens a condom and carefully rolls it on. He inches closer. She opens herself, and lifts her hips to aid his access. She lets him enter. She lets him be inside. That was his request: to be inside, a little while. Smooth and slow, she feels his hardness in her interior, the chafing despite his attempts to be gentle. She closes her eyes. The German holds himself up so as not to crush her, his hands firm on the mattress on either side of her body, but then he lets himself drop and runs his hands down her sides, taking his time, until he reaches the hem of her T-shirt, where her flesh begins, at her naked waist, and stops. Nat hears a soft grunt, senses the jolt of release, and lets him stay inside a little longer, as his body slackens. The rain has picked up again, plinking rhythmically on the shed's sheet metal roof. A cat miaows, pitifully, and the German pulls out, gets dressed, and leaves so she can clean herself up and put on her clothes.

When she comes out of the room, they don't discuss what has happened. Maybe silence, she thinks, is part of the agreement. She doesn't know if it was what he expected or not. So long since he'd been with a woman, he'd said, and now he has been with her. Did she meet his expectations? Despite the brief nature of the encounter, despite the distance between them, did he get the pleasure he sought? Brevity and distance, those were the conditions he had imposed. Maybe he thought it was less upsetting for her, or maybe his ground rules were a personal preference, a choice.

She is struck by a sudden, irrepressible need to know his name. Once, she heard him called Andrea, but she has her doubts because Andrea is a woman's name. Maybe it's Andreas, with an s that, here in La Escapa, no one is ever going to pronounce. Her understanding is that Andreas is a Greek name, but maybe it's also used in Germany. Is that why everybody simplifies things and just calls him the German? Nat won't ask. If there's anything she knows, it's that those kinds of questions are meaningless in the context of what has just happened between them. She pets the tiger cat – a female, it turns out – while the German – Andreas, or whatever his name is – looks for an umbrella to lend her since, though the rain is worsening, it goes without saying that she won't want to wait around. Or is he the one who doesn't want that?

He doesn't thank her when they say goodbye. As it should be, Nat thinks, this wasn't charity or altruism. Still, her chest feels tight and she wants something else. Maybe a small show of gratitude? Sure, that would be nice.

She can hardly sleep that night, bombarded by her own doubts. Did she behave like a whore? How is she to interpret what happened? How would a third party define it? If she'd received money at the time, cash money, if he had, for example, left it on the bedside table, would it mean something different? It would for her, since she doesn't want any money, she just wants him to fix the roof problem, which is, ultimately, the landlord's problem. But would the transaction not be the same if he'd given her money and, with that money, she hired a builder? Isn't that the same result? No, she concludes. Such a scenario would have just introduced more links in the chain – the money, the builder – elements that did not form part of their pact.

The absence of money – money that can be seen and touched – finally allows her to decide that it isn't prostitution. But her doubts persist. Isn't she looking for a way to justify herself, to make clean something which clearly is not? Does she actually believe that was a fair price for fixing a few leaks? Or had she simply waited for the rain in order to have an excuse? Had it been impossible for her to get the money any other way? If she had the money for Sieso's shots and vet visits, why didn't she have the money for repairs? If the landlord didn't agree to fix the roof, she could have threatened to move out. And done so. She has no ties to La Escapa. There are loads of similar places around these parts: oak groves, croplands, dirt roads. There's no shortage of cheap houses without leaky roofs.

She tries to view the situation from the outside. To see herself through the eyes of others, watching and judging her. No one would buy her rationale. Why should they? They would say she did it because, deep down, it was what she wanted. That she liked it. That, when it comes to sex, there's no grey area between pleasure and disgust: if she hadn't felt disgust, well, then it was clear what she had felt. Would it have been more dignified on her part if she'd been repulsed, if she'd felt upset or hurt, humiliated or used? If the encounter had lasted longer? Or if he had forced her to move, suck, bite, contort?

But the whole thing had lasted just a few minutes. So many questions don't fit in so little time. Maybe, she tells herself, she must confront it in a simpler way. The German made an offer. At first, she didn't think it was appropriate, but later, she did. She doesn't have to define the act with any term. He was sincere and clean. No hemming and hawing, no creepy advances like her neighbour's. The German expressed his needs, made his request, and offered something in return, something she truly needs. The encounter was as matter-of-fact as it should have been, not sordid or denigrating. She tries to remember it step by step, move by move. What did he say, with which words, at which exact moment? Repulsion or regret – what she might've feared – had not materialized. The German had shown sensitivity. A delicacy that, she must admit, she hadn't imagined in him, with his rough and not exactly sophisticated appearance. He tried not to hurt her, bearing his weight on his hands and going slow. She still feels the heat between her legs: heat considerably more mental than physical. Even though it was quick, the sensation that persists is of slowness. How can she explain it?

Now, she must avoid misunderstandings at all costs. He must not think there will be other opportunities, because there won't be. If some misunderstanding should arise, she will be firm. Nip it in the bud. The possible attraction of what happened between them – she later decides that the word attraction is a careless word, and replaces it with incentive – the possible incentive, she thinks, resides in the one-off nature of the proposal. Even if he were to suggest another encounter under the same terms, the circumstances would be wildly different: the body has memory, and to repeat is to reinforce. That's the last thing she wants.

The German arrives in his van the next morning and gets to work. Nat offers him coffee. No thanks, he's already had one. While he evaluates the damage to the tiles outside, she sits down at the computer.

'I'm here if you need me,' she says.

Then she thinks about the ambiguity of her words and is embarrassed. Nothing she could say is innocent now. This conclusion is irritating. It isn't a consequence she would have considered beforehand.

She finds it impossible to concentrate with him outside, so close by. It takes her hours to translate a single sentence, even the simplest ones. In fact, the simplest sentences put up the most resistance. The temptation to quit arises again. Why persist in doing something she's clearly bad at? She gets up once or twice to look at herself in the mirror: baggy-eyed and pale, not her best day, she thinks. She brushes her hair and puts on a little make-up. She returns to her seat. She perseveres, brooding at length over the same paragraph.

The German pokes his head inside, startling her. He says he's going to Petacas to buy new roof tiles, now that he knows exactly how many he needs. When he gets back, he'll have some work to do inside, too; he hopes it won't be a bother, he'll try to finish quickly. OK, Nat says, and a shudder runs through her when he leaves. Won't bother, will finish quickly: the same expressions he used the day before, spoken, even, with the same pronunciation, that incoherent crowding of syllables. Doesn't he know how to talk any other way?

The repair takes the whole day. The German water-proofs the surface, both outside and inside the house, and lays the new tiles. And a gutter, too, he explains, to channel the runoff when it rains to keep the water from pooling on the roof. Nat doesn't tally up the cost of the tiles, the gutter, and the waterproof paint, plus the few other products he has used, the purpose of which she is ignorant. All that plus the hours of work, the knowledge and skill required, is the price he put on her body yesterday afternoon. Is it a lot, is it a little? He hasn't said a word about it. He's said the bare minimum. He only breaks for a smoke, wandering around the property in complete silence. Nat thinks: he wants to leave me alone, he thinks I might be uncomfortable otherwise. But what really makes her uncomfortable is his reserve. So cold, she tells herself, and at the same time: what was she expecting? Warmth? It would be worse, much worse, if he were to do the opposite: to be affectionate or even suggestive, reminding her that he has had access to her innermost self and that such a step cannot be undone.

Her anger grows as the hours pass. She can't translate, she can't read, nothing distracts her. Even Sieso's presence is annoying. When she sees the German finally collecting his things, she considers offering him a beer, but he just leans inside the door to say goodbye – not coming in, not even crossing the threshold – and she drops the idea. He probably has better things to do, she thinks. His garden, for example. Or some other odd job, a repair like the one he just did for her, who knows. She says goodbye with detachment and only thanks him at the last minute. Although, she thinks, that's another mistake: she isn't the one who should be thanking him, but the other way around.

'I saw the German mucking about on your roof,' Píter says.

The words mucking about carry a subtle contempt, and Nat, feeling caught out, over-explains. He fixed a small problem with some leaks, she says. He didn't charge much and he did a good job, too, clean and quick. She blushes: clean and quick. Wait, she really had to pay him? Píter asks, scandalized. No, of course not, the landlord will take care of that. Eyebrow raised – an expression he often makes – Píter declares that the German does sloppy work. He doesn't understand why she called him when he – Píter – could have helped. A few leaks are easy enough to fix.

'I think he did a good job,' Nat insists. 'He spent the whole day. He put in a lot of hours.'

'That doesn't mean anything. Putting in a lot of hours is not synonymous with dedication. It can also be a sign of clumsiness. Or cheek: so he can justify the bill. How much did he charge?'

Nat stammers.

'I told you, I didn't pay.'

'But you don't even know what he's going to charge?'

'I have no idea, he made a deal with the landlord.'

'Before you said he was cheap.'

'Well, that's what I inferred. The landlord is such a cheapskate, it couldn't have been much.'

'The German and the landlord making a deal!' Píter clucks his tongue. 'I don't know how you trust them.'

Nat laughs and admits her mistake, but what's she going to do about it now? she says. She doesn't know if the German is a shoddy worker, but he's an odd duck, that's for sure. Why do they call him the German? Isn't his name Andreas or something? Andreas, yeah, Píter confirms. His mother was German, or Kurdish, or a Kurd living in Germany, he can't remember. Was he born there, in Germany? No, Píter doesn't think so, he doesn't know. He came to La Escapa about five years ago, he's never talked about his past. He's always on his own, does whatever jobs come his way and, yes, he repeats, he's sloppy. As far as he knows, the German has worked as a framer in Petacas, and as a delivery man, too. He repairs plumbing, does odd jobs, stuff like that. Now he works in his garden. Gets by on small things. But he doesn't talk to anyone, doesn't have friends. Píter doesn't buy the excuse that he's reserved. In a place as small as La Escapa, such isolation is suspicious. That – among other things – is why he says the German can't be trusted.

'What things?'

'Things. I don't know, things he does or I heard he does.'

'Things like…?'

'Oh Nat, I don't remember right now.'

'But if you don't remember, why did you just come out with that, like it was something really serious?'

Píter smiles, not a smile that inspires intimacy, but its opposite: the distance of someone who knows more or insinuates he does.

'Hey, why the sudden interest? What do you care about the German? You're, like, all defensive.'

Nat smiles too. Just curious, she assures him. He spent the entire day at her house, after all. And yes, one has to admit, his silence is rather peculiar. He barely spoke.

She's awoken by the sound of rain. It is a fickle, offbeat pinging, the drops falling on the gutter bought and installed by the German, the gutter he promised would channel water to the ground in an orderly fashion, preventing it from accumulating between the roof tiles. This sound transports Nat back to the day in his house when it rained on the shed's metal roof. Just as the rain started up, he'd run his hands down her sides – the only caress she got – from her underarms to her hips, from the fabric of her shirt to her bare skin, slow and gentle. She is startled by the memory. She turns on the light and tries to read, but it's no use. A chill runs down her spine. She feels anxious, like an animal in heat. What is happening to her?

At dawn, she returns to her translation. *Ce n'était pas une vision. J'ai touché ses cheveux…* The words echo in her head: hollow, mute, formless, until they begin to take on meaning, all possible meanings. Touch the mane or stroke the mane? Touch sounds bad, but it's what appears in the original text. If it was referring to caressing, wouldn't the author have written *caresser*? And mane? Why not hair? After all, isn't it more natural to stroke the hair, touch the hair? How would she say it? Touch the waist or stroke the waist? What difference is there between touching and stroking? She translates: *It wasn't a vision. I touched her mane*. Rereading it, she feels her revulsion grow. She stands and walks around the room. Sieso watches her, but the dog's gaze is not clear: there is judgement behind his eyes.

A couple of hours later, someone calls from outside, clearly pronouncing her name. The German is on the other side of the gate: patient, resolute, calm, in his work clothes and ill-fitting glasses. He's just coming to check that things are OK. With last night's rain, he repeats, was it OK? So that's it, Nat thinks. That's all? To ask about the work? She replies drily.

'Good, thanks. Tight as a drum.'

He breaks into a crooked smile: satisfaction for a job well done. That's what brought him here? Nat thinks. Nothing else? Really, nothing else? Doesn't he think he owes her an apology, an explanation, a sign of gratitude at least? Great, he says, just what I wanted to hear.

'If you have a problem, let me know,' he adds before turning back to the road.

Nat is frozen. Furious. She doesn't want him to go, yet she needs him to leave immediately. She detests his tone, the absolute lack of tact in his choice of words. If you have a problem, he said. And what about the other problem? She hasn't felt so bad, so wretched, in a long time.

What's he after, turning up at her house without warning? What right does he have? Everybody in these small villages does it, sure, but what a rude custom! She was relaxing – or trying to relax – she didn't want to see anybody, and she certainly didn't want to see him. But suddenly he appeared and she – hair unwashed, face unwashed, in her pyjamas – had to act like it was all perfectly normal, swallow her pride, and mimic a cordial and neighbourly coexistence after they'd made a simple transaction – sex in exchange for roof repair? Insane. The consideration, the respect, how's it going, everything OK with the rain, if you have a problem, let me know. He can't even tell I'm angry, Nat thinks. Not even. Two days ago he had her in his bedroom and now he just looks at her with utter disinterest, like he would look at a goat or a dog. Maybe he even regrets what he did to her, seeing her now, in the light of day. So long without a woman and all he got was her, that mess.

She runs into Joaquín and Roberta on her way to the shop. The old couple pick their way down the muddy pavement, arm in arm. Nat quickly catches up to them. They're not going anywhere in particular; they're just out for a stroll, or walking aimlessly. Joaquín says they need to stretch their legs. The doctor has recommended they walk: it's good for their health, physical, and mental, too, and he gives her a complicit wink. Roberta shows signs of recognizing Nat, smiles at her warmly and says a polite hello. But Nat senses that the old woman can't quite place her; she momentarily confuses her for the shopgirl, then with somebody named Sofía, who must be a relative. She speaks courteously, in an orderly way, with precise vocabulary and complex verbal structures, but what she says doesn't make any sense: there is a huge gap between the logic of her language and that of reality. Joaquín arches his eyebrows expressively, as if apologizing. Then Roberta asks about the dog.

'The dog?'

'Yes, the skinny dog. Is he better?'

Nat is happy to redirect the conversation towards safe terrain.

'I took him to the vet. He got his shots and he's eating good food now. I think he's even put on a little weight. But he still doesn't trust me. It's possible he was abused.'

'With the bricks.'

'With the bricks? I don't know what they used... rocks, or... who knows what.'

Roberta locks her eyes on her, which are ink-dark and clear.

'No! Not the dog! The German and the bricks.'

The German. She can't be mistaken. The old woman has distinctly said his name.

'What's happening with the bricks?' Joaquín says.

'Everything!'

She speaks with frustration now, wanting to be understood. She points a finger at Nat.

'She gives him the fruit and he lays the bricks.'

Nat is dumbstruck, mouth agape. The old man persists.

'The fruit? The fruit isn't the girl's. It's the German's. From his garden. He sells it. We buy it from him, too. Don't you remember?'

Roberta laughs softly, as if she has remembered something very funny. Muttering to herself, head bent, she repeats: she gives him the fruit and he lays the bricks. Nat tries to understand. Maybe the old woman saw Andreas going up on the roof, just like Píter saw him, just like other people in La Escapa will have done. Maybe by bricks she means tiles. But what does she mean about the fruit? The vegetables from the garden? Or something else? She shakes her head.

She shouldn't attach any importance to the words of a crazy old woman. It's Nat, Nat and her own susceptibility, that leads her to see everything from the wrong angle.

She turns up at night. But this time, it's not on impulse. She has thought it through and taken time to get ready: to shave, shower, wash her hair, blow it dry, put on perfume, pick out clothes she thinks are flattering. A part of her is aware of the contradiction in her preparations. If all she wants is to talk, to sort things out, to clarify the situation, or whatever, then all the grooming is unnecessary. But the two things are not mutually exclusive, she thinks later, as if defending herself before an intractable judge. She is nervous when she leaves the house, her chest tight. She takes the car because night has fallen and, for the moment, the neighbours' petitions for better lighting have not borne fruit. She drives slowly, trying not to make noise; her plan consists of suddenly appearing on his doorstep unannounced and getting her revenge. The silence, however, is absolute, denser and deeper than ever, and everything she does on arrival – park, turn off the engine, pull the handbrake – seems to echo, despite her intentions. Walking cautiously on the pebbled drive, she approaches the house and knocks, since there's no doorbell, at least not one she can find. Inside she hears the TV volume being lowered and then footsteps approaching. The German opens the door, looks at her in surprise and asks her to come in. Nat feels a jolt of fury and resentment at the sight of him, that obstinate, slow expression, as if he didn't get what was going on, and wonders if she's making another mistake. Her voice unnatural, she asks if she can talk to him for a few minutes. Sure, of course, he replies, and mutes, but doesn't turn off, the TV. He clears a spot on the sofa for her to sit – moves some cushions and shoos away the tiger cat – and asks her if she wants a beer, which she declines. He sits down in a ugly, frayed old armchair across from her. She does have time to notice that: the chair is ugly and frayed.

But they won't talk. Not then, not in the coming hours, not the whole night.

From that day on, the stream of her thoughts is completely redirected. Thoughts no longer flow where they used to. Now they go wherever they want, towards other places, and she can't rein them in.

It's like a movie playing in her mind. Parading images of Andreas, her and Andreas, Andreas and her, in bed. His body, her body, every movement, the wrinkles on the sheets, each one of the few words they said to each other. The movie ends too soon, it is desperately short. She rewatches it again and again, basking in the details, stretching each shot so it lasts longer, including prior scenes – her arrival at his house – and subsequent ones – their farewell, her leaving – although these last ones leave a bitter, murky taste in her mouth. It's still not much. Far from enough. Nat isn't quite sure why she wants to prolong the movie. It's a need she hasn't troubled herself to understand. She simply carries it with her, carries it everywhere, unable to disconnect from the images that have imprinted on her, inside of her, and now project through her eyes, everywhere she looks, anywhere at all.

Is it an obsession? Yes, it is clearly an obsession. But not only that, she thinks. It's a rapture, a metamorphosis, a radical transformation of the predictable. What was once outside, distant on the horizon, invisible and uninteresting, is now inside of her, inhabiting her, wracking her.

Hierarchies have changed. Everything is in disarray.

In order to explain it, she has to blame something outside herself, an external force. That first day, the day they made their strange pact, Andreas injected her with his poison. Yes, that was it. Nat had been unaware of his ploy, but when she dressed and left his house, she was already carrying it inside of her. The poison had continued to spread through her veins, flooding her with its dangerous effects. From that first day on, stripped of her will, she had no choice but to return: poison needs more poison, there is no antidote. She didn't choose Andreas, she didn't seek him out: he inflicted himself on her. She should resist, but it's impossible to fight: she's trapped. That's how she sees him now. It's her interpretation, a childish, magical interpretation – she is well aware of its flimsiness – but it is also tremendously useful for giving in.

Why resist? she asks herself. What does she gain? What is she going to lose?

She decides to go back again. And again. And again. The film reel grows, gets longer. It is never enough.

He is always willing to receive her. It's no longer a cold-blooded agreement, something that can be dealt with in five minutes. Now, they spend hours and hours together, they catnap, they start up again. They only pause to gather strength, until the time comes for her to leave, and even then, there is no ending, there is never an end. Nat has never known anything like it, not in this way. That man, Andreas, extracts something completely new from her, something insatiable and addictive. Aren't men supposed to slow down after a certain age? Andreas is tireless.

He is not, however, as voracious as Nat, or not as voracious as she would have predicted, given the circumstances. He doesn't demonstrate the exigency or tortured carnality she has observed in other men – no dark side behind closed bedroom doors. Nor the desire to prevail, to win that war, subtle and undeclared, which seems, on occasion, like impotence. Andreas's sexuality is that of a simple man, she thinks, a pacific man. The path they tread together holds no anguish, fear or obscenity, there are no misgivings or insults. Naked, lying side by side, they are like siblings. Nat doesn't have to chase her orgasm or desperately claw at its edges, begging to enter its domain. All she has to do is follow her body's signals, precise and pleasurable instructions that guide her to unmistakable success. Her body has instinctively gained such wisdom that it hardly matters that he's a stranger. Is it some secret knowledge, sacred and inaccessible, that unites them? If so, it's a religious connection, similar to what binds members of a cult, to the exclusion of outsiders: the profane, the novice, the ignorant.

And yet, when they finish, they cannot meet each other's eye and the shame and small gestures of distrust soon appear. Nat watches him in secret, fascinated by the body that has been hers and is now, suddenly, foreign again. Her own body also assumes another form, a contrary shape, as if the mirage of her agility and beauty dissolved in the emptiness, intimidated. When she pours a glass of water in the kitchen, her back to him, or when they sit across from each other under the citrine glow of the old ceiling lamp, their bodies are no longer allies, but adversaries again.

All it takes is a single touch, a new rapprochement, for the wheel to start spinning again. Irritation and desire, craving and vertigo: those are the alternating cogs.

Nat, the distant, impassible, aloof Nat, has transformed into a hungry creature. To such a degree that she has to stop herself from going to him at all hours, from falling asleep there at night. He has never asked her to stay and she convinces herself it's for the best: to preserve the spell of the illicit, see each other inconsistently, clandestinely. Even so, a part of her would love for Andreas to at least try to convince her to stay longer and there is always a residue of disappointment when she feels his eyes on the road as she walks away. He never tries to change her mind.

Sex? Is it a matter of sex? If she concentrates on what's below her skin, the tyrannical and insistent quiver, then everything points to yes. And yet, she refuses to reduce it to that. Sex has always been secondary to her. Pleasurable, sure – at times – but also pleasurably secondary: she could do without it no problem, she could forget it, even erase it from her life. Simultaneous curiosity and coolness: that's how it's always been. The men she was interested in were very different from Andreas. In general, she liked listening to their stories or taking walks, seeing a movie or getting drunk and laughing, much more than sleeping with them. She tired of all those activities eventually, but she always tired of sleeping with them first. Her body would close up at their touch, unbidden and disobedient. Frigid, she'd been called once, which was an accusation that applied to her whole personhood, not just her body.

When she was a kid, a man, a neighbour, had molested her on several occasions. Nat mostly felt confused after those encounters – a bit of guilt, a bit of fear, but confusion, above all – even though, as soon as she shook him off, she went on with life as if nothing had happened. The man would sit her on his lap and rub himself against her. He didn't hurt her. He was a good man whom Nat's parents were very fond of, an old man – Nat remembers him like that, old, though he probably wasn't much older than fifty – a music lover, solitary, with small, kindly eyes, whose wife had died of cancer several years before. Nat couldn't speak badly of him to her parents, she didn't feel she had the right. And even though she started avoiding him, she was also fond of him, in her own way. Had all of that conditioned her developing sexuality? Nat doesn't think so, despite what they say about cases like hers, all that stuff about the indelible mark of childhood. But even if that were true, even if the neighbour had turned her into a detached, insensitive person, now, unexpectedly, all that has changed, thanks to another man.

*

Píter has been calling her nonstop. First Nat says she's busy, then that she doesn't feel well, she has a terrible headache, her neck and back hurt too, it's not good to be sitting for so long, translating. Her excuses are clumsy and rude, she knows it, but she'll explain everything to him later. However, days go by and she doesn't find a good time. Until one evening, when she is just about to leave, Píter appears at her door.

'Sight for sore eyes!' he says.

He looks her over, smiling, but scowling, as if trying to solve a riddle. Does she have time for a beer? he asks. He's on his way to do some shopping in Petacas. She could come along and they could get a drink, how does that sound?

Nat doesn't answer right away. Suddenly, an offer so simple, so ordinary, is hard for her to handle. She shakes her head. Another time. Another time? he laughs. He's come to see her a few times now and she's never in. What does she have to do that's so important? She's dressed and everything, she just has to grab her purse. She doesn't even need to bring any money. His treat. Or is she on her way somewhere else?

'I was just going to take a walk.'

'Take a walk with me!'

'No, seriously, another time. I need some time alone.'

He raises his hands in a sign of peace. Cool, he says, he doesn't want to bother her. That's never been his intention. He thought she could use the company, especially if she's spent these awful days lonely and in pain, as she says. Or maybe she's had other company? Maybe she hasn't been that lonely.

'You don't have to hide anything from me.'

Unease slithers through her. Píter's voice contains no notes of reproach; the opposite, really, he's been sympathetic and kind, playful about a situation where friends would usually give each other a hard time. But underneath is the sense of moral obligation: Nat shouldn't lie to someone who has been so good to her. She says she's sorry. She admits she owes him an explanation. She promises she'll explain later, as soon as she can. Píter puts out a conciliatory hand. It's OK, he says, fingers stretching to rub her arm. Unconsciously, Nat recoils.

'I really have to go. I'll tell you everything soon, I promise.'

'The details, anyway.'

'What?'

'I mean, you'll tell me the details. I already know the basics.'

'Of what?'

'You and the German.'

Nat goes blank as Píter smiles, sardonic. The basics? Does he mean her visits to Andreas – her private, repeated visits – which must have reached his ears? Or what's behind it all, too, their roof agreement?

Sieso observes the scene from a few metres away, hieratic, ears pricked, his eyes slits. Anubis, she thinks fuzzily: maybe she should call him Anubis, the embalmers' jackal, a god of strange physiognomy, but still a god. Píter shakes her from her trance. Seriousness has returned to his full, mild face. He strokes his beard thoughtfully as he speaks, as if in deep reflection, underscoring the weight of his words.

'Honey, this is La Escapa. A handful of houses in the middle of nowhere. What did you expect? That no one would find out? All I want is for you to be OK.'

'I'm OK.'

'That's all I want. If you're OK, then I have no opinion. Forget what I said last time.'

'What do you mean?'

'Last time, when you asked and I told you I didn't trust him. You were trying to get me to talk, weren't you?'

She blushes, though Píter hurries to clarify, again, that he isn't upset, he completely understands and has no objections, just as long as she's OK.

What is it with all this insistence? Are his words a warning? When Nat bids him goodbye, it's with only light concern, barely significant because, at the moment, her urgency to leave – her desire – outweighs it.

But later, those ounces of suspicion will begin to multiply, to take on heft.

'Did you like me right away?'

No, Andreas says. He doesn't hesitate. He doesn't even pretend to think about it: a categorical and impassive no. Actually, he adds, he hardly noticed her. He saw her out on the roads, or in the shop, but she didn't spark his curiosity. He's very inattentive. It always happens to him, with everyone. Nat feels a pain in her throat. Harsh and sharp, well-aimed. Inexplicable. She struggles to swallow.

'So, I could have been anybody.'

It's only mid-afternoon, but the light in the bedroom is murky, as though it were already dusk. They can barely make out each other's faces. Andreas deliberates for a few seconds and then looks up at the ceiling.

'You could be someone else and so could I. That's how it always is.'

'But if I hadn't come looking for you after... the first time, none of this would have happened?'

'Maybe not.'

'It really hurts to hear you say that.'

He smiles absently.

'It shouldn't. In the end, it happened. You are you and I am me. That's what matters.'

Nat would like to ask what she means to him. She would like to say that, if everything started by chance – a chance as petty, as trivial, as a leaky roof – then she doesn't get why they keep seeing each other, since their agreement was fulfilled. She knows it's ridiculous but, deep down, she would like to be the chosen woman, to have been seduced after careful planning. She would like to hear that Andreas noticed her from day one, fell in love slowly, over time, concocted plans to get close to her, saw his chance and jumped, never mind the risk: the romantic narrative replacing the... pornographic? But Andreas says none of this. He just looks at her seriously, as if her pain was contrived and he, at most, should be charitable and overlook it.

'Well, did you notice me?' he asks at last. 'Isn't it the same thing?'

Nat turns towards the wall to hide her tears. It all started in that very bed, she thinks, when he told her to strip from the waist down if that's what she preferred. He used her because the prostitutes in Petacas were, he said, awful. How should he know? Had he resorted to them on other occasions? Tired of the whores' wretchedness, he decided it was better to approach her? What kind of person does that?

Andreas moves closer, rubs her back, kisses the curve of her neck. Can't she be content with the facts? he says. The facts on their own? Why does she need to interpret everything? What does she hope to achieve? Nat doesn't respond. Lying on her side, arms crossed, she tries to expel the devil that is taking her over.

On Saturday, she wakes to her neighbours' voices in their yard. They must have arrived the previous evening and now are frantic with party preparations. Nat hears them talk about pork chops, charcoal and lighter cubes. The children fight over a toy in high, exasperating little voices. Nat covers her head with a pillow. It was very late when she got home from Andreas's, waiting until the last minute for him to ask her to spend the night – waiting to refuse the invitation – and now the ruckus will keep her from getting more sleep. She gets out of bed but doesn't decide to do anything in particular. Her translation is on the table where she left it, a page reflecting on silence, *de notre silence en particulier, une qualité de silence en particulier*. But if silence is the absence of words, how can there be a silence in particular? Shouldn't all silences be the same, like the colour white is always the same? So, what differentiates silences are their surroundings, obviously, starting with the causes. Andreas's silence when sex ends, is it the same as hers? Nat senses that it is not, that it is made of other stuff.

She hears Sieso bark and goes out on the porch. Píter is by the gate. His magnificent dog wags her tail at his side, drooling with excitement. Nat and Píter haven't mentioned Andreas again. They, too, have chosen a kind of particular silence. She promised to give him more details, but on second thought, what sort of details can she give? The details are gratuitous. They could even be counterproductive.

'I'm taking these over to The Cottage,' he says, holding up a case of beer. 'See you over there.'

'Over there? What do you mean?'

'The autumn party, the party to celebrate the...'

He sets the beer down, pensive. That's weird, he mutters, rubbing his temple. They didn't invite you? Every year, her neighbours throw a party to welcome the autumn. It's a La Escapa tradition, he explains. They must have just forgotten.

'Want me to remind them?'

Nat vehemently shakes her head.

'What do I care about that party? I don't belong there.'

But Píter looks displeased. He insists on mediating. It's important that everyone in the community get along. When he says community, his eyebrows rise, solemnly.

'Well, I'm sure I'm not the only one they didn't invite. I'm sure they didn't invite the gypsies. Or Roberta. It's not like they're obliged to invite everybody, are they?'

'Oh, come on,' Píter protests. 'That's not the same.'

'Yes, it is. And it would be worse if it weren't. Even less reason to go.'

Nat, truthfully, doesn't care about her neighbours. She feels contempt when she sees them acting like The

Cottage is actually a beautiful home on a beautiful estate. She derides the invisible pressure they put on themselves, and their children, to look happy all the time. And yet, a part of her – an amphibian, or reptilian, part – is intrigued that they have excluded her. Why? How has she upset them?

She feigns indifference in front of Píter and later, too, when she tells Andreas about it in a fit of uncontrolled loquacity. She isn't offended, she claims, although she is surprised to be excluded like that. They probably reject her way of life. They must not approve of her living there alone, of the fact that she doesn't have a husband to mow the lawn, that she's over thirty with no kids – and no plans to have them – that she doesn't worry about La Escapa's sewers or the strength of the local school system, which they debated with so many of their friends last time. They've almost certainly found out about Andreas, about her – she hesitates, looking for the right word – friendship with him. They must find that condemnable, as well.

'Can't it be that they simply forgot about you?' Andreas interrupts.

Nat feels like she is being accused of something, though she isn't sure of what. Being a drama queen? A victim? Self-centred? No, they didn't forget, she says. That's impossible. They live right next door, their properties abut. And they've invited her before. No, she just has to accept that they don't like her.

'But you don't like them either, right?'

'Of course not.'

'Would you invite them over?'

'I wouldn't even have a barbecue.'

Andreas smiles.

'Then what do you care. You're speaking different languages.'

By now, the whole of La Escapa knows the deal with her and Andreas. As Píter warned her, in such a small place, in such a limited community, it would be naïve to think they hadn't all been talking about her for days. She notices how the girl acts differently when she goes to the shop: cooler, distant, like she's been slighted. Her mother, who used to come out of the back to say hello, clearly avoids her, pretending to be busy in the storeroom. In Gordo's bar, she has to deal with the whispers and glances of the construction crews from Petacas, appraising her on the sly. Nat is disheartened. Why does everything have to be so hostile, so complicated? Even her landlord seems to know something, or she imagines he does. The day he turns up to collect the rent, knocking ostentatiously on the front door, he snidely points to the gutter.

'Whoever did that really knew what he was doing.'

A thought crosses Nat's mind, like a shadow. Maybe the landlord knows about more than her relationship with Andreas, maybe he knows the terms on which it was established, the chain of causes and consequences that, if put into words, would sound forced and even preposterous. But the landlord doesn't go on. Nothing about the possibility of discounting her rent to cover the repair. No thanks, either. He just takes his envelope and asks about

Sieso. How's the beast? he says. The beast. It's a word Nat
has encountered often lately, while translating. Bête, though
here its meaning is different. Disrespectful.

'He's great.'

'Yeah? Guess I have to believe you. I never see him.'

'That's because he hides.'

The landlord guffaws.

'Hides? So he hides now, does he? And who does he
hide from? Me? That's rich!'

'I didn't say from whom. I just said that he hides. He's
a solitary dog. Does his own thing.'

Does his own thing: a conclusive statement, proud, one
that gives the dog some dignity. It would be fairer, more
appropriate, to say that Sieso is surly, bad-tempered. But
that would mean making a concession to the landlord,
ceding in the struggle taking place between them on another
level, behind their words.

'Is that why you tie him up at night, because he does
his own thing?'

Nat pales. How does he know that? Does he prowl
around her house at night? She cannot answer without her
chin quivering. Like when, as a kid, she was caught in a lie.

'I tie him up because I don't want him to get into fights
with other dogs. They all go crazy before the sun comes
up, all of them barking at the same time.'

'Crazy? Girl, they're dogs! What do you want them to
do? They're dogs, full stop. The worst thing you can do
to a dog is tie him up. A dog needs to make his rounds.
Fuck around and look for bitches. If you don't leave him
loose, then he really will go crazy.'

Fuck around, look for bitches. Is that what he does when he hangs around La Escapa at night? Nat feels a pit in her stomach, her legs go weak. If only she had the strength to throw the man out that very instant. Tamely, she waits for him to leave.

She studies Andreas's behaviour meticulously, his tone of voice, the way he sits beside her or leaves space between them on the sofa. She registers, like a person taking scrupulous inventory, the times he touches her hand or looks at her – even fleetingly – the way he focuses when she's telling him something, the inflection in his voice, scouring it for amiability or impatience. It's never enough. She feels, for instance, that when they drift off in bed, he pulls away too soon, or holds her for only a short time, before turning over and immediately falling into a deep sleep that excludes her completely. She watches him and thinks: how does he manage it? How can he forget about her presence right there beside him? Nat dozes off and on, just for a few minutes, from pure exhaustion, only to startle awake, heart pounding, distressed to discover they aren't touching, that each one is on his or her own side of the bed, no contact at all.

The same thing happens with food. Nat has a lump in her throat that makes it hard to swallow; even chewing is an effort. In contrast, she sees him eat with gusto, discarding her the instant he spears with his fork or cuts with his knife, focused only on his utensils and plate. Nat wonders what goes through his mind then. Does he forget about her entirely, does his hunger cast her aside?

The contrast feels brutal: she can't detach from him for even a second.

Sometimes, she feels real rage. Her own personality has been evicted so that he can occupy her completely and she, submissively, has let him enter. But him? What has he given her in exchange? He appears to be impervious to everything, and barely allows contact. If she tells him something personal, he listens to her in silence, making no comment. He doesn't ask for details nor does he try to interpret the events. The respectful attitude, which she finds lacking in other people, is frustrating coming from Andreas. Can she chalk it up to his character, so cautious and reserved? Perhaps he doesn't want to appear to pry? Or is he just not that interested? He doesn't talk about himself much, and when he does, it's only in reference to external things, insignificant subjects, far removed from the two of them. His anonymous and anodyne tone makes Nat feel strangely humiliated, as if she were chasing somebody who wants nothing to do with her, jogging ridiculously behind a person who doesn't even know she's there.

Other times, however, she lets herself be carried away by the headiness of the moment and believes she is going to burst with happiness. Holding his hand, still dazed, recovering from pleasure, she feels as though a cyclone has knocked her down and dragged her off to another world. When Andreas gets up, she buries her face in the sheets, tracking the scent of his sweat, practically in tears, repeating his name in a whisper. There's no greater union between two people than what they have, she tells herself. Maybe he's right. Maybe it's better not to delve into the mystery, not to try to understand it, so it doesn't get ruined.

The ache of happiness is an idea that haunts her now: a kind of happiness that, within it, contains the seed of its own destruction.

One day, she asks him what his cat is named. Li, he says. Li? Just Li? Yeah, L-I. The cat doesn't need a last name, does it?

'Why Li?' she persists. 'Does it have a special meaning?'

'No, not at all.'

'It's pretty,' she murmurs, just to say something, dodging the sense of having made a mistake, though she can't imagine what she did wrong.

It's hard to get anywhere with Andreas. Whenever she asks him something, his answers smack of closure, a pre-emptive sign that it is futile to go on. Maybe the strange thing about his speech is not, as Nat thought, the crowding of syllables, but the unequivocal tone, self-sufficient, that underlies his pronunciation.

Furtive, she watches him as he lies on his back, his eyes closed, resting. When he finally falls asleep, she props herself up on her elbow so she can study him more closely, greedily. She looks for traces of previous generations in his features – the Kurdish, the German – the ones she doesn't know about because he never discusses his past. She reads his face and in it she finds a distinct majesty: his face is exactly as it should be, she thinks. Taken separately, his individual features lack beauty; they are, in fact, even common: the hooked nose, the lips tucked under the coarse, greying moustache, the violet shadows that make his eye sockets even more pronounced. But she is captivated by the combination as a whole.

One must watch him like this, like she does, to access that face which is out of reach for others. Decisive, hard, full of secrets. It is a disconcerting face.

It is impossible to get at what's behind his eyelids.

Andreas has been neglecting the garden as of late. Even Nat, who knows nothing about plants, can see that. Maybe he hasn't needed to water, not with all the rain, but one can't simply rely on the weather: a good part of the vegetables are going bad precisely because of the excess water. Plant pots full of puddles, rotting sprouts, branches gone wild, twisting out of control, dirt dug up by the cats that come in to steal Li's food... this is her view of the garden now. Since they've been together, Andreas only picks vegetables for his own consumption. He no longer distributes produce to the neighbours, at least not to her knowledge. When she asks, he waves his hand: an unconcerned, or maybe apathetic, gesture. The garden isn't important, he says. I was planning on quitting it sooner or later.

'Well, it would be a shame. Everything you grow is great.'

Andreas nods. Yeah, it is. Or was. But it's time to do other things.

Other things? At first, Nat believes he is referring to her – to the time he spends with her – but her intuition is quickly steered in another direction. She is on alert.

As he rolls a cigarette, Andreas explains that a friend of his – an acquaintance, he corrects himself – set up a land surveyance company in Petacas last year. He ran it on his own at first, but he's already put together a modest portfolio of clients and now needs more people. So he's going to work with him, as a topographer. He's actually going to start next week, in just a few days. He doesn't have high expectations but, no matter how small the village, the town administrators all brag about their urban development projects and public works. Basically, it will be that kind of work: a steady drip of small jobs.

Nat has been listening to him, mouth agape, surprised to hear terms she never would have imagined coming from him, expressions like modest portfolio of clients and urban development projects. Wasn't Andreas just a country guy? Now, suddenly, one must presume that he's educated, has a degree, culture, all the things she hadn't expected. A flurry of doubts arise within her, questions she wants to ask accruing behind her teeth. What, exactly, do topographers do? Measure the terrain? Draw maps? What kinds of instruments do they use? Tape, levels, compasses, GPS? Who do they work with? Public works, construction companies, businesspeople? She simply can't imagine Andreas handling official documentation or writing reports. The mere possibility of him using a computer seems exceedingly strange. He doesn't have one at home and even his mobile phone is strikingly rudimentary.

Her question comes out of the blue, unexpectedly violent.

'But did you even go to school for that?'

Andreas looks up, observing her seriously. A wrinkle marks his forehead when he replies.

Of course, he says. He studied geography in Cárdenas, longer ago than she would believe. Is she surprised? What does she think a topographer should look like? Did she really think he was only good for planting lettuce? He laughs, but his laugh comes from far away, from a place she has been thrown out of. Nat apologizes and goes outside. She crouches down and pokes in the dirt, doubtful. Píter didn't tell her any of this. He simply said Andreas was a sloppy worker, disdainful of him. Did Píter not know, or had just he pretended not to? She is besieged by a thought – a malicious thought, very unlike her: Andreas is trying to get away, all of this is a lie, nothing but an excuse to escape from her. Is this actually happening? Is she going to show up at his house one day and he won't be there? He'll spend hours away, supposedly working, while she paces, hot with desire, waiting for him? Silently, she digs around in the dirt, catches a worm with her fingers, red, shiny and wet. She is so taken aback that it doesn't even disgust her. She lets it crawl over her hand.

The new job means they see a lot less of each other than before. Andreas is scheduled to work in the mornings only, but sometimes – more and more frequently – he's gone the whole afternoon. Nat continues to go to see him at the end of the day, when it's getting dark. They go to bed, they have dinner, then she goes to sleep at her house, scrupulously observing the new routine that has been established between them. He barely tells her anything about what he does in Petacas, about his work, but she doesn't ask, either; she doesn't want to seem nosy or stupid, and a strange caution – strange but understandable – leads her to choose silence. They talk, sure, about other things, usually in bed or while making dinner, but it is conversation that only tiptoes, beating around the bush. As the days go by, a new habit emerges: they have dinner first, then go to bed. Nat registers the change with disappointment and a slight but sharp pain. It signals the loss of urgency, of the desire that was so pressing, so fierce, that possessed them both in the beginning and which did not tolerate delay. Now, Nat thinks, hunger for food is greater than the hunger for their bodies.

Andreas's distance weighs so heavily on her that she believes she cannot bear it. Completely incapable of translating, the idle hours become fodder for suspicion. In an effort to stave off those thoughts, she offers to give old Joaquín a hand looking after his wife and their house. They come to a quick agreement: Nat will go over a couple of times a week and will also bring them their daily shopping. On workdays, she will help Joaquín bathe Roberta, wash the floors and dishes, do the laundry, and cook for them. They can't pay much, but something is better than nothing.

She also goes to Píter's for distraction. They pick back up with their early sociability, though now, to avoid certain subjects, they stick to the trivial and entertain themselves with movies or word games, the kind of humour that makes Nat laugh like a little girl. Contrary to what she might have expected, Píter doesn't reproach her for having abandoned her intellectual labour – the translation he praised so highly – for the dull, utilitarian work of looking after an old couple. In fact, he approves of her decision because it signals her idea of community. Nat doesn't know if his opinion is sincere or if he just wants to placate her, but she is conscious of the fact that her friends in Cárdenas, or her family, couldn't bear to see her like this, as a cleaning lady, or the help, as her mother used to say. Is this where all that studying has got you? they would ask. Waiting like a bitch in heat for a man she barely knows, bathing a half-mad old lady, sleeping alone, her only companion a dog she still has to tie up at night. What kind of life has she chosen? Was this the goal of all her supposed rebelliousness?

One day, she gets carried away and falls glibly into confessional mode. She tells Andreas what she told Píter the first night she had dinner at his house. The story of the job she quit. The motiveless theft. Her rejection of compassion and reprieve, her pointless pride. It is, perhaps, Andreas's mute response that paradoxically encourages her to continue, to use progressively imprecise and spacious words: words like guilt, absence, confusion, vertigo. Andreas makes no reply and she keeps talking, lost in abstraction, lying on her back, staring at the ceiling, at the naked light bulb she knows like the back of her hand, that dusty bulb and black wire.

The weight of the silence is only evident when she stops speaking – the stale air, Li purring at their feet – and Nat becomes aware of Andreas's slow breathing, his stillness beside her. Suddenly, everything – the bedroom, the cat, her own body – seems unreal to her, toy-like, small and insignificant. She even thinks he might have fallen asleep, but his eyes are wide open and vacant, indecipherable.

'What do you think about all that?' she asks.

'All of what?'

'What I told you. You're so quiet. What are you think-ing about?'

Andreas sits up and gives her a hard look, there is a new opacity in his eyes – glass eyes, dead eyes. His voice is dry and unexpectedly severe.

'Are you just asking to ask, or do you really want to know?'

For an instant, Nat thinks he's joking, but when his inert eyes and creased chin do not soften, she knows he's not joking, not at all.

'Have you ever stopped to think about other people's lives? About the actual worries people have?'

'What? How is that related to…'

'It is related. It's totally related.'

Like a child ordered to parrot back what has just been explained to him, Andreas repeats her story. In his voice, in his words, it all sounds flimsy, a triviality bordering on the grotesque: she had a good job, she stole something without knowing why – something that, supposedly, she didn't need – she was forgiven for her mistake, but even so, she chose to quit her job and come to La Escapa, where she ended up with another job, after all, because now she goes to the old couple's house and they pay her for it. Is that right?

'Yeah, more or less,' Nat says coolly.

'And you think you have a right to complain?'

'Complain? That's not… You've misunderstood.'

'Don't you know there are people who steal out of neces-sity? Who lose their jobs without the slightest justification?

That this happens to people every day? That they get fired because of a simple oversight? They forgave you and you're still complaining?'

'I'm not complaining! I was talking about something else!'

'What were you talking about, then?'

But she doesn't know how to respond. The man lying beside her, the naked man with whom she has just exploded in pleasure, is now an armed stranger. He, who never gets upset, speaks then of his mother, as if he needed to get angry in order to expose an intimate piece of himself. He tells her that she was Kurdish, from northern Iraq. When she was very young, she was forced to flee from war – one of many – and go into exile in Turkey, travelling on foot for days and nights with a baby – him – in her arms. Later, she suffered hunger and hardship in Germany – he'll spare her the miserable details – and still, he says, his mother never stole anything. She was a good woman, brave and generous. She never spoke a word of complaint.

'I'm sorry,' Nat whispers.

'What are you sorry for? That my mother suffered or that you've been complaining about nothing?'

'I'm sorry about your mother. But it seems like you're blaming me. My story has nothing to do with hers.'

'Nobody said anything about blame. It's simply a matter of being grateful. When you snatch something, you're already thinking about snatching something else.'

'What are you talking about?'

'I mean in general. That's how you are.'

'You don't know me that well! How can you say that?'

'You asked me what I thought. You wanted to know, you said. Well, that's what I think. Don't take it as an attack. In the end, they're just my thoughts.'

Nat is about to cry. An ungrateful cry-baby? That's what Andreas thinks of her? Is she really like that and never realized? She deeply regrets having spoken because, as a result, she has gone backwards, lost points. Now Andreas has seen a part of her that repulses him. And she's going to lose him because of it.

On the bed, between them, she feels the opening of an abyss.

They go up El Glauco, in Andreas's van. He suggested the drive – it's Sunday, his day off – a proposal that Nat interprets as the recognition that, between them, there is something that extends beyond the bedroom walls. It feels strange to be with him outdoors. Suddenly, walking beside him seems more intimate than getting in his bed or undressing in front of him. To feel him next to her, driving, also leaves her deeply flustered. She shivers with desire when she watches him changing gears – his fist around the gearshift, the fingers that touch her busy now with another instrument. She admires his profile, his droopy glasses, the line of his nose, gruff and proud. She lets herself be carried away by a fierce, gluttonous joy, though she simultaneously attempts to pump the brakes; by now, she can recognize the kind of joy that ends in anguish. Like when your legs stop working after a long run, she thinks.

They take a very narrow dirt road which ends at a lookout point. They leave the van parked and climb the last stretch, up a steep and slippery slope flanked by thorny bushes that snag on their clothes with every step. Nat's calves get scratched, she feels tiny insects swarming around her head, a constant and maddening buzz, she is out of breath and tired. At no point does Andreas hold out his hand to her. He walks a few metres ahead, determined, never once looking back. Nat's elation has completely vanished and she wonders what they were missing by being here. In a different time, they wouldn't have wanted to leave the bed, they wouldn't have wasted the hours this way. Now they need field trips?

But the effort is worth it. From up high, Nat takes in a view she never could have imagined: the fields around La Escapa studded with little white and dun-brown cottages, farmhouses, farms, a broken stream that shines in some places. The beauty of distance, she thinks, and allows herself to imbibe the mountain smell, the hawthorn and elderberry, the rosemary. They kiss and he strokes her cheek.

'You're beautiful,' he says.

Nat looks at him, suddenly grateful. But Andreas's eyes are already absent, distant behind the lenses of his glasses, and the buzzing continues around her head, as though it were coming from the centre of her brain. A few kestrels circle overhead; Andreas squints to make them out. They're hunting, he says. They can stay like that for minutes, soaring until they spot prey, but he says it to himself, murmuring. They look down over the edge of a steep drop-off and she thinks: we're alone, he could push me and make me fall, leave me out here, injured, with no chance of getting back, nobody knows I'm here, nobody would miss me. The thought is a blunt attack, like it didn't come from her. Maybe it's because it's an outside assault that it feels so plausible, so near.

Andreas offers her water from the canteen.

'It's cold,' he says. 'You need it.'

Has he sensed her fear? Grateful again, Nat drinks, and as she drinks she feels like she is being cleansed, that the water washes the poison of foreboding from her throat. She is on the verge of apologizing, but why bother. He would never understand.

Nat has almost forgotten about the landlord entirely when he next makes an appearance at her house. He looks at her as usual, staring at her body, her breasts, making a show of his power and boorishness. Nat doesn't have the cash ready. She usually stocks up at the ATM in Petacas, but this time she forgot. She apologizes. She tells him she's been very busy with work. She didn't expect him so soon. Time is flying by. He looks at her sideways, purses his lips until they disappear.

'Well, your buddy goes to Petacas every day. He could have got the money out for you.'

Her buddy – an oblique allusion, full of poison, that Nat cannot respond to.

None of this would happen if he would just allow her to transfer him the money like everybody else. Or at least warn her before he shows up, not like this, out of the blue, waving the bills, as if she had nothing to do but wait around with the exact amount in cash in an envelope. But she will only think of these arguments later. What dominates now is the landlord's expression. His lips thinning in a sneer. The glint in his eyes. Arms crossed, smug.

Nat apologizes again and tells him to wait a minute. She turns away and calls Píter to ask for the money she needs. Although she speaks quietly, the landlord overhears their conversation.

'They eat right out of your hand,' he grumbles.

Píter is at her disposal. If she wants, he'll run the money over right now. Nat hesitates a moment. She doesn't want him witnessing how the landlord speaks to her, how he imposes his humiliating conditions.

'No, don't worry. I'll come to you,' she says, and hangs up.

Then, mustering the courage, she asks the landlord to come back in a little bit. Fifteen, twenty minutes max.

'I won't be long.'

'I'd better stay here, that way I can rest.'

Nat tries, unsuccessfully, to speak. Her head is starting to spin. The landlord laughs.

'What, don't you trust me?'

He sits down on the sofa and looks around the room with a tight smile on his face, observing everything with a clear intention of making her see him do it. Nat doesn't argue. She rushes out.

'I'll be right back,' she says again.

She is still shaking when she returns. The landlord indulgently counts the notes, folds them slowly and tucks them in his shirt pocket. Nat feels like the house is steeped in his smell, an acrid odour, unpleasant, hanging heavy in the air. When he leaves, she checks that he hasn't touched anything. Everything appears to be in order, except, perhaps,

UN AMOR

a couple of magazines he must have flipped through. Her bedspread is wrinkled, but maybe it was already like that, she can't remember. She tosses the magazines in the bin, throws the bedspread in the washing machine on hot, and spends the rest of the afternoon cleaning with the windows open, airing things out.

Despite the minimal attention she now pays him, Sieso is much changed. Nat no longer ties him up at night and he repays her trust with loyalty, sleeping on the floor beside her bed. Maybe she should start thinking about changing his name, she thinks. For as ironic and even affectionate as she intended the name to be, the meaning of sieso is bad-tempered, rude, a nasty piece of work. And the vet already warned her: animals don't understand irony.

On the other hand, she thinks, maybe it isn't worth it. Most people don't even know that meaning. The term sieso is only used in certain spaces and circles; its usage is more limited than Nat initially believed. She thought it was a well-known adjective because she knew it, frequently used because she used it frequently. She wasn't aware of its limitations until she realized that even Píter didn't know what it meant. Later she confirmed that its colloquial meaning isn't even included in the dictionary. The entry lists only the scientific definition, much more unpleasant than expected: 'From the Latin sessus "seat" 1. Noun. Anus with the inferior portion of the rectum.'

But if nobody knows, then who cares?

It's just a dog's name.

*

113

Li goes around and around the house, unsettled, her miaows sound different, low and pitiful. Nat observes her, notices that she's got fatter as of late. Could she be pregnant? she wonders, and later asks Andreas. He chuckles.

'Wouldn't be the first time. When my ex-wife left her with me, she promised the cat was spayed. But as you can see, she's getting chunky again.'

Nat is stricken. His ex-wife? Has she heard correctly? The wind rattles the shutters, warning of the coming storm. The first drops are already plinking off the shed roof and a sudden darkness surrounds them. She must not allow that sound and that light – those memories – to be ruined. For something that once meant one thing to come to mean its opposite.

Andreas is fixing the TV connection. The screen on the antiquated set, which they now occasionally watch during dinner, is always beset by wavy lines that distort the image. Perhaps because his back is to her, possibly because he is focused on something else, Nat dares to press.

'So, Li isn't yours?'

'Well, uh, at this rate I don't think anybody is coming to get her.'

'I didn't know you were married.'

'Well, how would you?' He turns to grab a screwdriver. 'That was years ago. Before I moved out here.'

'So... what happened?'

'What else... the usual. We didn't understand each other. She was really young, I was way older, more than twenty years, I think, and she wanted stuff I couldn't give her.'

'Like what?'

'Just stuff. I mean, in general. Stuff like trips, kids. Stuff I don't care about. So she got sick of it and left.'

Nat sits on the sofa and pets Li as she watches him take the TV apart. Li. If the cat wasn't his, if she had belonged to his ex-wife, then the woman had obviously picked the name. Now she understands why Andreas told her it didn't mean anything, when in reality, it meant everything. Why didn't he tell her the truth back then? The stab of jealousy, so swift and unexpected, makes her ashamed: she always thought she was exempt from such a petty feeling. And yet, who pulls the strings of her suffering now? Who decided that something like this – the past of a man she barely knows – could wound her so badly, overshadowing her own convictions and ideas?

In a vague way, she feels duped. What led her to accept the roof exchange was a vision of Andreas that is now completely muddled. She was attracted to the impression she had of him, an image he himself might have wanted to convey, of a country bumpkin with no possibility for change, a man who hadn't been with a woman – he said so himself! – in a long time. A man who had lost his ability to seduce, if he'd ever had it, and found himself obliged to propose an exchange of goods, as if he lived in a primitive settlement, ignorant of the rules of common decency. A man who perhaps never left the village, and when he did, it was only to haul crates of the vegetables he grew. A crass man, uncultured, who'd lived in the country since childhood, adapting instinctively to any turf like an abandoned dog. A man who simply – who only – made one clumsy, humble request: that she let him enter, like a beggar on a doorstep.

His inexperience had elevated her, made her powerful. His lack was, for her, his riches.

But that man had a university degree. He had lived in a city for many years. He had been married. Married to a very young – and presumably attractive – woman. He got divorced. He had followed life's usual path, observed the usual rites. Then why is his way of relating to her so unusual?

The first thunderclap splits the air as she observes his damp neck, the way he fiddles with the cables. She swallows. What else can she say? He doesn't seem very willing to explain.

She focuses on trying to control the thoughts taking root inside her, to cut off their limbs as best she can. Since she met Andreas, everything has gone completely off-script. Dismantling all of her prejudices, Andreas digs into her defencelessness, removing her confidence by the shovelful. She becomes increasingly small, while he, in contrast, is stronger. He is freer, she more dependent. She can't handle another surprise. This is why she is afraid to speak.

That day will be the first that she is unable to avail herself of desire in order to forget. The first time she must conquer her thoughts while they take off their clothes, force herself not to lose heart. The first time her body struggles to respond and she exaggerates her pleasure. The first time sex becomes something sad, bitter and oppressive.

Píter opens a bottle of wine and serves her a little, but Nat, preoccupied, is slow to take the glass, as if she didn't quite understand what the glass contained nor why she's holding it.

Píter jokes, tries to get her to come around. Weakly, she follows along. What was very funny before – his silly jokes – she now finds dull or just plain stupid. Why is she there, in his house? Just to kill time before she goes to Andreas? Píter inspects her closely. Is everything OK? Yeah, fine, Nat says, all good, but her tight smile tells a different story.

To confess her malaise, she thinks, would be to validate a prediction that Píter has never actually made. Or has made surreptitiously, which makes it all the more complicated to refute.

If she considers the facts on their own, abstaining from parallel interpretations, objectively she has nothing to complain about. What's she going to say? That Andreas was married? That now he's working in Petacas? That one day – just one time – he accused her of being ungrateful when she asked for his opinion?

To express her pain – her ridiculous pain – out loud would only make her more vulnerable. Yet not talking, keeping it all to herself, doesn't make it go away.

They're sitting on the porch, protected by the glass partition. El Glauco's outline softens in the twilight; soon the darkness will swallow it whole. Nat fixes her eyes on it, the mountain that, not long ago, she and Andreas climbed, trying to keep sight of it in the twilight. Píter sets out smoked salmon, a plate of cheese, cured meats, and spicy potato salad in colourful bowls. He is always so obliging, so sensitive! Andreas has never made her a dinner like this. He wouldn't make it for anybody, not even himself.

Nat breaks down, speaks nervously.

'Did you know Andreas was married?'

'Me? How would I know? That guy is practically autistic, he never tells anyone anything. How do you know? Did he tell you?'

'He mentioned it the other day, by chance.'

'I seriously doubt that he says or does anything by chance. He'll have told you for a reason, looking for something.'

Nat is quiet. Better to end the conversation, she thinks, before Píter starts dropping hints. But now that he's taken the bait, he isn't going to let go so easily.

'What did he tell you?'

'Not much. That she was younger. Like, by twenty years.'

'Twenty years!' Píter whistles, then laughs. 'Check out the German!'

Nat is immensely hurt by that whistle. To hide it, she immerses herself in her glass, knocking back the rest of the wine. She shouldn't have spoken, but there's no taking it back now. The only way to stop the conversation is to invent an excuse, to get up, and go.

'Hey, what's wrong? Are you angry?'

Repeatedly she denies it, grabs his hand to prove it, assures him nothing is wrong. But what about dinner? She's going now, without a bite? He doesn't care what she says, it is simply not normal to up and leave like this.

Nat knows it. She knows her behaviour is erratic and rude, incomprehensible from the outside, or maybe the opposite, all too transparent. But she can't stop. She's certain she has begun a descent. And her only option is to keep going down.

She wakes at midnight, suddenly, and can't fall back to sleep. She remembers Andreas's words, which now, in the silence, become more and more cutting. Way older. Stuff she wanted and he couldn't give her. Stuff like trips, kids. Stuff he doesn't care about.

Compared to Andreas, Nat had come to believe she was powerful. She liked to think that, at twelve years her senior, he'd been seduced by her youth, that it elevated her, increased her market value. But this had been another miscalculation.

She has always considered it an undeniable fact that men, regardless of their age, are attracted to younger women. But until now, she'd never interpreted that as a threat: no matter how young you are, someone will always be younger. She had never thought in terms of competition. Now she does.

She thinks about the girl from the shop.

Sometimes Andreas drives her to Petacas in his van, where – supposedly – she places orders or collects merchandise ready for pick up. The girl from the shop is very young, practically a teenager, but by the looks of it, her age isn't a problem but a bonus. Nat remembers the heat Andreas gave off when driving. The desire he can awaken simply by changing gears – the taut forearm and strong fist, gripping the gear stick – his eyes jumping from the rear-view mirror to the road, the hard eyes she can never get past.

The intimacy of the van, the dense air and shared cigarette smoke. The girl isn't pretty, but she does exude a seductive audacity and, most importantly, she's dying to escape, she's bored and anxious to try new things. Might he, when the time comes, also ask her if he can be inside her a little while? Might he have already asked her, maybe even before Nat? If all Andreas needed was a little female warmth, wouldn't the girl also do? Even better, in fact? Did he stop because she was underage? And if she weren't?

Nat can't understand why Andreas offers to drive her to Petacas. Andreas, who is so distant with everyone, makes an exception for the girl, as if supplying the damn store was his responsibility. Nat draws her conclusions and feels cold – an intense cold that radiates from her own insides, from a spot somewhere between her spine and breastbone.

Why is Andreas with her? Because he hasn't found anything better? Because she's what he has on hand?

Once one certainty has crumbled, can't they all?

Her internal gaze has turned wary and she can no longer curb it. I'm going crazy, she whispers, and looks with burning eyes around her dark room: a private space that does not protect her, but turns on her, and stabs her in the back.

She remembers that recurring dream, the one with the man who entered her house while she was tied, defenceless, to the bed, the man whose face she never manages to see. Maybe he didn't represent the landlord, like she'd thought. Maybe it was an omen of what was to come.

Her relationship with Andreas has been tainted from the beginning. The way it began, a way that once enthralled her, a way that has been turned inside out, showing its repugnant seams.

It's not as though she was innocent and pure before, but at least parts of her – leery, malicious parts – had been dormant. They're awakened now. The damage grows, branches off inside her.

When she is cleaning out the old couple's storage room, Nat find several boxes of books: mostly schoolbooks and literary classics, but also a few news-stand novels that must have been popular decades ago and which, nowadays, nobody remembers. Joaquín explains that Roberta was a teacher for forty years, the better part of them in the primary school in Petacas. The books are hers, he says, or rather, they were. She hasn't been able to read a single word for a long time now; that's why she's decided to take them off the shelves and pack them away, out of her sight, so they won't torment her.

Nat studies Roberta, so fragile and confined to her own world, so hermetic, and it's hard to imagine her having another life. Roberta, working with kids, going over a lesson on the blackboard, subject and predicate, addition and subtraction? Nat flips through her books, annotated, underlined, bookmarks made of construction paper and pressed flowers – had Roberta made them? had her students? – and her chest tightens.

What does Roberta think about, what does she look at? She always appears deeply focused on something occurring in another dimension, her eyes squinting and her lips forming silent sentences. Who is she talking to?

Sometimes the spell breaks and the woman comes back to herself. Then she discovers that she isn't alone and tries to be pleasant with the people around her. She might speak nonsense or get frustrated when they don't understand her, but she is a polite woman, and never makes a scene.

One day, she receives a call with dire news. A relative, a nephew perhaps, is dying. This is what Nat deduces from overhearing Roberta converse, eyes lowered, twisting the phone cord around her fingers. Afterwards, she spends several hours deep in thought, picking up – then hanging up – the telephone, although no one is calling. When Nat asks Joaquín, he shakes his head and says Roberta has made it all up. There is no sick nephew, nobody is dying. It happens a lot, he says. She gets fixated on things from the past. In the old man's resignation, Nat also senses a hint of despair. What will happen when he isn't there to take care of her?

Joaquín is going blind. He confesses this to her one day, in tears, his head on his fists, seated at the kitchen table. Nat is moved to see a man cry, a man that age.

Joaquín and Roberta form a fissure in the community; they are, in a way, as anomalous and defective as Nat. It's hard to see, hard to look beyond, it isn't pleasant. But once she makes the leap, she can no longer feign her innocence.

The afternoon is overcast. The still air is charged with static electricity. Buzzards fly low, soaring over Nat as she walks towards Andreas's house – an unusual direction for this time of day. She knows he isn't home. She doesn't know why she took this route and not another – she hasn't stopped to consider this – just like she doesn't know why she decided to go for a walk, even though it threatens to rain at any moment. Intuition perhaps, a hunch? That's what she will tell herself later when replaying the events. Now she just walks, her thoughts elsewhere, until his house takes shape in the distance, and there, at the gate, his parked van. She stops. It takes her a moment to comprehend. Or try to comprehend. Her temples pulse wildly, a flash of heat rushes to her face. She turns abruptly on her heel. It's better if no one sees her there.

She gets home and tries to calm herself. There must be some explanation. A reasonable explanation, she thinks: Andreas has returned to La Escapa because something came up, he had to pick up a tool or forgot some equipment. Or maybe, maybe, there's something wrong with the van and he took a different car this morning, or got a ride with someone else. She feeds Sieso, opens a beer, lies down. But she gets right back up. The explanation could be very different: at that exact moment, right now, Andreas could be in his house with another woman. Another woman he's duped with the same ruse he used to dupe her.

She leaves her house again and walks quickly – now in the rain – towards the shop, her breathing ragged, until she can look inside and see the girl behind the counter, texting on her phone. Nat's relief at the sight of the girl is so great that she laughs, but her laughter, too, is short-lived: if it isn't the girl, it could be anyone.

Or maybe it's nobody. But if it's nobody, why didn't he call her right away, like they used to? Doesn't he have the urge to see her? Isn't he dying for it like she is?

She spends the whole afternoon walking back and forth between their houses. The van is always in the same place. It hasn't been moved. At the sight of the white smudge, she turns around and begins a new loop. Her heart is beating so fast that it scares her. She has never done anything like this, not even close. Nothing so grotesque, so undignified.

She lets the phone ring when Andreas calls her that night, ignoring the calls until he tires of trying. She would have liked him to try a little longer, to not give up so easily, but even so, to ignore his calls feels like a secret revenge. She feels she's won, although what battle?

The next time they get together, they both act normally, or what constitutes normal for them now. He doesn't ask why she didn't answer his calls. She doesn't ask why his van was parked at his house all day. Since there are no questions, there are no answers. Nat's mistrust continues to grow: subtle and twisted, like a cat's cageyness. And his? If it's mistrust or simple disinterest, she couldn't say.

She makes a habit of spying on him after that. She pokes around the area near his house, watches the van's comings and goings, compares timetables. She scours for indications of possible visitors. Finding nothing, she thinks: he's careful, he destroys the evidence. When Andreas isn't watching, she inspects everything she can get her hands on: food jars, medicine, bottles. She keeps track of how many condoms they use and does her maths. She examines the papers that lie scattered around the house – invoices, commercial notices, advertising flyers, receipts. She finds some old CDs and sneaks them out to secretly review them at home. They just contain blueprints and topographical reports, but her anxiety is not quelled, she keeps searching. In his wardrobe, she discovers dress clothes, nicer than what he usually wears – she has never seen him in a suit, but there they are, irrefutable, jackets and ties. Two additional discoveries produce deep misgivings: a receipt from two years ago from a women's clothing store in Cárdenas – woman's shirt 39.90 – and a little musical jewellery box with a tiny ballerina that, when the lid is open, turns and turns to the tune of 'La vie en rose'. Nat shuts it, not wanting to give herself away. She wants to smash it.

Checking his phone is not very rewarding because he hardly uses it. All she finds are texts from her, spam messages, and calls sent and received from the same numbers, which belong to his associate in Petacas and some supposed client. The fact that Andreas always leaves his phone out, freely accessible, and that his contacts are so limited might mean there is nothing to fear. But it could also mean the opposite: that Andreas is faking, that while she sneaks around, he is sneaking around too, erasing numbers and compromising messages and leaving the phone within her reach, all to mislead her.

Nat always chooses the worst of all possible interpretations. She's never safe, not even when she convinces herself that her ideas don't make sense. Any variation, any nuance she hasn't foreseen, as slight or remote as it may be, makes her reel. Jealousy, that relentless green-eyed monster with its pointed tongue and obscene sneer, slips into bed with them, probing them, ready to devour them, poisoning the meaning of their movements, staining them with baseness and suspicion. Why does Andreas close his eyes when he's with her? Is it because he's thinking of someone else? Because he's remembering his young ex-wife? His dark eyelids, his concentrated expression and the light tremor of his lashes, everything that Nat admired in the early days, what turned her on, now confirm all her suspicions. Nat, threatened with frigidity, has also started to fantasize. She dreams up scenarios in which other men ask of her what Andreas asked. They do the same thing to her – exactly the same – that he did the first time, under the same darkness and in the same silence, and she is naked only from the waist down, and there are no caresses except their hands running slowly down her sides. They perform like Andreas, but are not Andreas, because Andreas isn't who he used to be either: he is a different man who is likely behaving like she is, keeping her at a distance even as he touches her, pushing her away the deeper he delves into her body. When they finish, they are silent, not with their early shyness, but sadness. Are you cold? he asks, handing her a blanket. You can't imagine how cold, she wants to say, remembering how he used to wrap her in his arms. Now he only wraps her in courtesy – clumsy and hurtful.

She hardly ever goes to Petacas now, just for quick trips to get money from the ATM, as if the town – already a hostile place – was prohibited to her since Andreas started working there. But one day, consumed by wild conjecture, she decides to go with the excuse of getting a haircut. She tells Andreas ahead of time, in passing, so he doesn't get any ideas if he sees her around town. Andreas looks up, observes her in a way that makes her feel exposed.

'But your hair's fine. Why do you want to cut it?'

'I have to get a trim. I haven't cut it in ages.'

'I think you look fine.'

This comment, which could be considered a compliment, is interpreted by Nat as a sign of detachment: Andreas doesn't want her to show up in Petacas, he doesn't want to have her around. But she can't back out now. It would be even weirder to renege: a clear confession.

She goes early and parks in the first spot she finds. Since she doesn't know where the hairdresser is, she ambles along, avoiding the mud collected along the pavement. And it's just when she reaches the town hall square that she sees Andreas talking to someone, vigorously waving his arms, as if he were arguing, smoking while speaking, tilting his head back to blow out smoke, legs slightly apart. They are gestures Nat doesn't recognize in him, and even his body, seen from a distance, looks unfamiliar. The man Andreas is talking to is taller than him, and younger. Much younger, actually, which turns Andreas into another person, practically an old man. For a moment, Nat feels an urge to retreat and hide, but she steels herself and walks towards him. As she gets close, she can tell the men are not arguing; they are simply talking the way men talk sometimes, with that mix of sarcasm, camaraderie and crudeness. He turns, sees her, and smiles. His smile doesn't mean, however, that she is welcome, and he immediately disengages from his interlocutor, as if he didn't want her to come any closer.

He doesn't introduce her. He says a quick goodbye to the other man as his smile fades.

'What are you doing here?'

'I'm getting my hair cut, don't you remember?'

'Oh yeah, that's right. Where are you going exactly?'

'Nowhere in particular. I don't know where there's a salon.'

'Come on, I'll show you one.' He sets off walking a few steps ahead, glancing around as if looking for somebody else, as if she were the odd one out or as if she weren't even there. Nat follows him with a heavy heart. Andreas hasn't kissed her, obviously, and hasn't come close enough to touch her either, yet just a minute ago, she saw him with his hand clapped on his friend's shoulder.

'Look. Here's where I work.'

Though the door of a small establishment, Nat glimpses an office crammed with papers, pieces of equipment, and boxes, with a couple of computers and a giant printer in the centre of the room. Andreas's colleague – a man the same age as him, with dishevelled hair and wearing a tracksuit – leans over a couple of blueprints so big they drag on the floor. He doesn't seem worried that they might get creased or dirty. Andreas waves to him from the door. He doesn't go inside and doesn't invite her to go in. He raises his arm to point down the street: the hairdresser is that way, he says, two or three blocks down. His tone is so curt – or so it seems to Nat – that it accentuates her interloper status. When he says goodbye, he squeezes her arm and looks her in the eyes, but this isn't enough for Nat now.

She's an outsider at the salon, too. The hairdresser, with her long curly mane, tight T-shirt and strident laugh, is straightening a client's hair when Nat walks in. The woman doesn't put down her tools or ask what she can do for her; she asks her – orders her, more like – to take a seat and wait. This is what Nat does, wait, while she tries to read a book she's brought. With her eyes glued to the page, she listens to the conversation between the two women, who criticize someone with tacit comments and private jokes. Their complicit laughter makes Nat uncomfortable, as though they were laughing at her, too – and who knows, she thinks, maybe they are. When it's her turn, the hairdresser scrutinizes her in the mirror. She asks how she wants it cut but doesn't pay attention to Nat's instructions. She inspects her hair, lifting clumps and carelessly letting them fall. It's really damaged, she says, a lot needs to come off.

Nat doesn't reply. She lets the woman do what she hasn't asked for.

The new style has added on a few years; she even looks paler and more puffy-eyed than before. Despite telling the woman that she didn't want bangs, she has them now, parted in the middle. But she smiles and pays what the girl asks for without complaining.

Before leaving for La Escapa, she stops at the indoor market to shop for the old couple. In line, she observes the chatterbox women and foul-mouthed men: the cryptic way they speak, at breakneck speed, completely foreign to her. A pair of stray dogs sniff around the boxes, undisturbed. She has to keep an eye out because as soon as she's distracted, someone cuts in front of her and takes the best produce.

Even the children – shouldn't they be at school? – look crafty and sly. And the teenagers have an arrogant glint in their eye, defiant.

It can't be so horrible, she tells herself. It's her, her way of seeing things, that's sick. If only she could shut her eyes and see no more.

She hasn't thought of her in years. But, thanks to the hairdresser episode, it unexpectedly returns: the memory of those luminous days and how they later turned sad and baffling. Nat was seven or eight at the most; Estrella must only have been a few months older, although at that age a difference like that constituted a big advantage, since it was a privilege to be the friend of, or to enjoy the favour of, an older girl. She can't remember her face or voice, but she does remember how the girl sat behind her, brushing her hair. Estrella dreamed of being a hairdresser, but she couldn't practice on everyone, she said, just her: lucky Nat, chosen from among all the other girls, the one with the softest hair, she claimed, the longest and prettiest of all the locks. She did braids and little buns, she brushed her hair for hours, blew softly on her neck to tickle her, and Nat closed her eyes and let herself be handled. One day, she started to yank, pull her ponytail much too tight. Your hair's breaking, the girl would say, and she would throw the brush on the floor in a huff. Nat didn't understand what mistake she had made, she begged the girl to try again and, if she hurt her, she silently held back her tears. After a couple of days, the girl had replaced her. From her corner, Nat watched her brushing the chosen girl's hair, combing with extreme care, tying it back with colourful elastics, doing little braids around her forehead – things she had never done with her – taking the girl's chin to admire the finished product, joyfully clapping her hands. The new girl observed Nat from afar, a little uncomfortable, perhaps, but helplessly gratified.

Nat didn't know what sin she had committed to be punished like that. When she saw a picture of Adam and Eve expelled from Eden, she thought: that's what's happening to me.

Her neighbours are unloading bags of food from their minivan while the kids run around, dragging a bow and quiver of coloured arrows. Despite the fog and distance, Nat has the impression that the wife is pregnant. The man waves and she feels obliged to go over, to be polite. They ask how her week has been. They complain about the storm, the wind that took down the thatching on the porch roof. They are unexpectedly cordial again, affectionate even. It's as if she's only interesting when they can smell trouble, she thinks. As if they sensed that things were falling apart for her and were happy about it. The woman takes her arm and, yes, she confesses, she's pregnant. Her eyes shine as she says it, grabbing Nat with the closeness one uses with female friends, and invites her over for dinner that very night. To celebrate, she says. Before Nat can reply, the woman changes her tone and lowers her voice. Stroking her belly, she adds: the invitation is just for you. Nat doesn't understand at first.

'I mean... we wouldn't like it if the German came.'

'Andreas?'

'That's right, Andreas.'

'Of course,' Nat nods. 'No problem.'

The wind picks up, cold and biting, almost hygienic. A gust that puts an end to the possibility of rebutting, or at least asking. A gust that draws the conversation back to the weather, what a pain. But Nat wonders: why the prohibition?

Going to dinner will mean not seeing Andreas that night. Accepting the invitation will then become a message to him – a covert message whose contents aren't clear, even to Nat. She decides not to do any explaining. She simply sends a text to let him know, they'll see each other tomorrow. How will he interpret that offence? The most likely thing, Nat believes, is that he won't interpret it at all.

At night, during dinner – Píter is also in attendance – the neighbours detail their plans to build a pool on their property. They've run the numbers and it's not that expensive. They want a long and narrow pool, so they'll be able to swim comfortably. A functional pool, even if it isn't pretty.

'The worst thing about a pool is maintaining it,' Nat says. 'A nightmare.'

They nod, they've considered all the drawbacks, but they're still going to put one in.

'I don't know,' Nat says. 'I've always thought they weren't worth it. Sorry, but I think it's ridiculous, with so much water wasted every year...'

'You don't drain the water every time. There are products to keep it clean. Products and covers.'

'Yeah, harsh chemical products... I'm not into them, either.'

Nat is talking rubbish and she knows it. She knows nothing about pools yet here she is giving her opinion. What's wrong with her? Does discussing pool mainte-nance help her contain her urge to get out of there and run straight to Andreas? Píter comes to her rescue and changes the subject; she focuses on her meal and recalls her neighbour's words – her attitude, the lowered gaze, the hesitation in her voice, her hand rubbing her belly – we wouldn't like it if the German came. Myriad possibilities flood her mind. It occurs to her that Andreas might have had some kind of run in with the neighbours. Or maybe just with the wife, something private, something intimate. After all, she made that plea when her husband wasn't in earshot. He wouldn't have asked her to let him enter... Her face tightens with pain. Píter watches her from across the table. No, she tells herself, it couldn't be. The neighbour used the plural – we wouldn't like – so that can't just be the reason. She could ask Andreas himself and eliminate her doubts the easy way. But she won't do that. Andreas is not the least bit affected by what other people think of him. If she tells him what happened, he'll just say it doesn't matter, or might not say anything at all. He would never get mad, even if he knew they were going around speaking ill of him. Or letting slip insidious insinuations.

Nothing is more out of character for Andreas than anger. Nat has never seen him get worked up or lose his cool, like she just did over the subject of the pool. He doesn't raise his voice, not even the day he talked about his mother.

And he never argues. He expresses himself without her need – her yearning – to be understood. He doesn't carry any desire to convince.

Strangely, this attitude makes Nat more uneasy than reassured. She wonders if his neutrality is not also some invisible method of attack.

They're in bed when they hear Li miaowing. The miaows are deep, long laments. The cat circles through the house, entering and exiting the bedroom, caterwauling incessantly. Nat's thoughts are miles away and she senses that Andreas's head is also somewhere else. But the noise isn't the only reason. Something in their bodies has ceased to work and cannot be repaired. They go slow, are stiff and awkward in their movements. Nat thinks about how different it was just a few weeks ago, when they held each other and everything was liquid and flowing. That thought – that comparison – makes the situation worse. And then there's the cat, the plaintive cat who continues to wail like a baby – more maddening than a wailing baby – ceaselessly, demanding, much more intense than usual, much more insistent. Nat stops.

'Could she be in labour?'

'No,' Andreas says. 'She's looking for the babies. They were born yesterday.'

Nat sits up. She looks at his face. He isn't wearing his glasses. He looks vulnerable, but distant.

'Well, where are they?'

'I drowned them in a water barrel.'

'You drowned them?'

'What did you want me to do? It was the best thing for them.'

Nat is horrified. Why drown them? Was there no other option? He didn't even consider another option! Why couldn't he keep them? He has more than enough space! Or give them away? Doesn't he regret having killed them? Doesn't he feel the slightest compassion? As she asks him all of this, she gets dressed, making a show of her indignation, though she herself knows that the dead kittens aren't her only reason for being upset. Andreas doesn't answer. He gives her a long look of contempt before asking her if this is how the night's going to end, if she's just going to leave in the middle of things, if she can't control herself at least a little. As if he cares how the night ends, Nat retorts: he's the most insensitive person she has ever come across. Not only when he's killing babies, but always. When she leaves, he'll probably just start watching TV like nothing happened.

He stares at her, undaunted, his pupils vacant. He slowly gets dressed, and carefully puts on his glasses before speaking. In every one of his movements, the end is foreseen. In the way he ties the laces on his boots. In the way he adjusts his belt buckle after he has fastened it. In the way he looks up at Nat, bringing her into focus, repeating the words she's just said: killing babies, what bunk. She thinks she has the ability to understand and the right to judge. But she doesn't know anything, he says. She should shut up a bit. Take a look around and shut up.

Nat bites her lip. She answers, holding back tears.

'You sound like my landlord. The same disrespect. You both think you're better than everyone.'

SARA MESA

'Because your landlord's right. We have different rules out here. And you don't understand them. It's not that you don't accept them – you are incapable of understanding them.'

'What rules? What rules are you talking about? Trading labour for sex, for example?'

She doesn't have time to regret it. She's said it and it is unforgivable. Andreas pushes her away with his arm, and looks at her harshly. From the edge of the bed, he sighs deeply, smooths his hair, and says, with complete calm, that he wants to split.

'Split what?' Nat asks, shaking.

'Split up. End whatever this is between us. Break up. Whatever you want to call it.'

'I didn't even know there was anything between us!'

'No? What do you call coming to my bed every night?'

'I've been asking myself the same thing: what is this?'

'You've never got it, have you? That's why you spy on me, circling my house to see if I'm home or not... Because you just don't get it.'

'What are you talking about?'

'You know what I'm talking about. It's over. You've exhausted my patience.'

Nat hears the words without catching them. She perceives the sounds but doesn't grasp them. Something has started to change inside her. Her rage dissolves and makes way for a hollow whose echo thunders throughout her entire body. She has fallen into a well and is drowning. She rubs her eyes with her fists, looking at him from a distinctly different place now. Her voice – her own voice – sounds remote to her, as if she was a dummy, speaking words that come from very far away, outside herself.

'No, no, no. You're not serious.'

Andreas doesn't answer. A profound stillness overcomes her: she is out of the game. She stays a little longer, paralysed, now sitting on the floor, one shoe on and one shoe off, her blouse still unbuttoned, waiting.

'You'd better go,' Andreas says after a few minutes.

Nat stands up, finishes getting dressed, and leaves.

Or rather, she must have stood up, dressed, and left: later, she won't remember doing it, she's like a sleepwalker. Neither will she remember what she says when she goes – if she says anything at all – nor how she walks back; how, because of the darkness, she almost has to feel her way forward, stumbling; how she opens her front door, throws herself face down on the bed and crushes herself against the mattress, attempting to suffocate her suffering.

Sieso comes to the edge of the bed, rubs his muzzle gently against her face, then lies down on the rug beside her. Now, with the exception of that dog – the guardian of the dead – she is alone, completely alone. Surrounded only by silence: the usual fictitious silence. A four-wheeler's engine drills the air, a couple of dogs bark in the distance, and coming towards her, some new words make their way: time is the punishment. She speaks them aloud as if she was reading them, as if they didn't come from her, but from beyond, way, way beyond.

She calls him the next day, and the next, and the next, refusing to believe that he will keep ignoring her, each time promising herself that this call will be the last, aware that she is playing into his hands, basely kneeling, and even so she persists; she's ready to appear at his house or show up at his studio in Petacas if necessary. Andreas answers on the third day, only to reiterate his decree: they must stop seeing each other. He says it calmly, surely. He doesn't get upset. He doesn't yell. He doesn't admonish her for the previous calls, the harassment. Her doesn't admonish her for anything. In the absence of hysterics, Nat knows his decision is irreversible.

But she cannot accept defeat. She begs. Pleads. He cuts her off. From now on, he will never answer another of her calls or reply to any texts. Andreas's resolve, his coherence, Nat thinks, resides in that: not letting his arm be twisted, not going back on his word.

The knowledge that he has reached his limit makes her literally sick. She gets into her bed and doesn't leave it for days. She keeps her phone close, checks it every five minutes, stashes it under her pillow and feels around for it, overcome with fatigue but never quite falling asleep. Her skin burns with despair, refusing to admit it has lost Andreas, his body, everything they did and will never do again. She goes over what happened again and again, the words they spoke, the order in which they said them. He shoved her away – pushed her with his arm, almost knocking her to the floor – he expelled her from his house. It's so horrible, so heartrending, that she wants to scream at the memory of it.

Píter comes to see her. He is worried about her confinement. What's wrong? Has she been to the doctor? Does she need something? Nat doesn't waver, she won't let her arm be twisted either. She just asks that he explain to the old couple that she can't look after them for a while and that he buy some food for Sieso. How ironic, she thinks: Píter will take charge of feeding the dog he detests.

He must mention the state of her to the neighbours, because the wife stops by to say hello on Friday. She brings a selection of herbal teas neatly presented in a wooden box, each infusion recommended for a different ill. Chamomile, lemon balm and linden blossom, sage, thyme, valerian and mint, easy remedies for digestive issues, insomnia, aching bones, menstrual pain, even sadness.

'The box is for you. You can keep it, it's a present.'

A malicious present, Nat thinks, a suggestion that she will eventually be afflicted by all those maladies, but she thanks her for the gift. The neighbour makes light of it. That's what they're there for, she says, to help each other; she knows that Nat would do the same if the situation were reversed. Nat observes the burgeoning bump under the neighbour's indigo cotton dress. She looks at the woman as if seeing her for the first time and notices how much more attractive she is than when they met; her hair is silkier, her skin more youthful, she displays a natural elegance that suddenly makes Nat feel very uncomfortable. Almost unwittingly, she asks her point-blank:

'What's up with you and Andreas? What's your problem?'

It sounds much ruder than she would like. An aggressive question, she thinks: now the woman will feel attacked and won't give her an answer. But the neighbour bows her head as if carefully considering the question. But when she looks up, she denies it with a smile.

'Nothing. Nothing is up.'

'But you forbade me from bringing him to your house!'

She keeps smiling, unruffled.

'"Forbade" is a bit intense. I just asked you.'

'But why?'

Again she pats her belly, swaying.

'No reason. I just don't really know him.'

The husband comes to visit in the afternoon. He offers to bring her whatever she needs, do whatever she needs. Is her appearance really that concerning? Or do they suspect the real reason and delight in her pain?

The husband's voice harbours an inappropriate, hopeful note. Does his wife know that he's there? Did she send him, or did he think of it on his own? Nat stares at him and notices how he dithers, as if he wanted to say more than he does, with his liquid – liquified – eyes and a few meaningfully prolonged seconds.

The neighbour doesn't know how to smile without including a smirk of deceit. Or if not deceit, of slyness. For a moment, Nat thinks that they're both of the same stripe.

She has nightmares that leave her exhausted. Sometimes, all she has to do is nod off for a few minutes, at any time of day or night, and in this short span, a whole legion of beings appear in her dreams – faceless people, talking animals – to address her, order her about, or lock her up in dark, labyrinthine places. When she wakes, she looks around her and the bedroom seems completely foreign. Every piece of furniture, every object, is in its place, yet something has changed. She can sense it in the atmosphere, like a slight dip in temperature, or the fading colours of an old photograph. As though the world had decided to keep moving forward, mutating, while she has been left definitively behind.

She hates the house so much! How fruitless were her efforts to improve it! Her attempts to make her mark through cleaning and decorating have been futile. Her belongings sit there as if they'd been cut and pasted from somewhere else, a poorly executed collage. She looks at the table with her papers, laptop and books, at the curtains she sewed for the kitchen, the old copper candle holders – so lovely – the ceramic fruit bowl. All of it grates. Everything has grated from the beginning, she tells herself: she does not belong to that place, she has never belonged.

Two full weeks have passed. It's another Sunday. Now it's her turn to make a move, though she doesn't know which move to make, nor in which direction.

She goes out for a walk.

She turns onto the dirt trail that leads to the old couple's house, through orchards and fenced-in plots with chickens and pigs. She can make out the two of them in the distance, sitting under the arbour where grapes are still growing fat. She has abandoned them, she hasn't even stopped in to see how they are doing. Should she? Yes, she should, but later. She contemplates the blossoming orange trees. Unheard of, Píter explained to her, such late flowering, the result of that autumn's unusual heat. Nat wouldn't call it heat herself, but atmospheric stagnation, as if the air had stopped circulating, fossilized at mid-height, not around her feet or face, but at her hips, impeding her progress.

She is alone. Sieso followed her for a couple of hundred metres, then stopped in the middle of the path, watching her as she pressed on, ignoring her whistles, before heading back with his ungainly trot. Now Nat approaches the orange trees, discovers that their leaves are plagued with aphids. Some, completely infested with the critters, curl up over themselves, dried out. The pale sky is yellowed from a column of smoke that rises in the distance. It smells like smoke and orange blossom and also like manure, all mixed together. A little further on is the incestuous siblings' house with its red graffiti, god's punishment and shame. Nat peeks through the window openings – the frames stripped and panes removed – and into the interior, which is filled with rubbish and flies. She enters the dwelling even though she knows there's nothing to see – nothing good – and there, inside those walls where the air is thick, she is overwhelmed by an unbearable conviction. Her actions are futile, it doesn't matter what move she makes: she will never get Andreas back.

She has lost him.

She had him and she lost him.

That certainty rends every single muscle in her body. She believes she will die of pain, she believes it is possible to die like this, alone, among the ruins of that house. She almost falls to her knees, but she contains herself. Leaning against the wall, she tries to control her breath. She has the sense that she's witnessing the last scene of her life. This is true suffering, she thinks. Something terrible is going to happen, she thinks next.

A little later, on the way back home, she detects the commotion: initially, a few figures, out of focus, and then people standing around, moving around something, a dust cloud raised by a couple of cars – the neighbours' minivan starting up – and shouts muffled by the distance. She quickens her pace as a dark premonition burgeons inside her. She keeps moving, although she doesn't fully understand, even if now the cries belong to specific people; they belong to the neighbour woman jumping into the moving vehicle and to the little boy, throwing a tantrum at being left behind. There is, in addition, a group of two or three men; one of them holds a stick – something that looks like a stick – and prowls Nat's property. The minivan is already gone, its shape almost indiscernible in the dust. What's wrong, she wonders as she hurries, what's happening, then she sees one of the men running towards her, calling to her, his tone is not one of warning, but accusation, as if she were guilty of something, hey, he says, hey! he yells, and all the rest comes very quickly. It's the dog, they say, that savage animal. Where had she been? The girl's face is destroyed, they say. Why did she leave him loose? Doesn't she know he's a beast? And where is the demon now? She has to turn him over, they say, they'll make short work of him, that poor girl, she should see her, see what her dog has done. Nat struggles to follow. She looks at the boy, who stands at the door, holding his face in his hands – fingernails scraping his cheeks – screaming in terror, and she sees a woman – the shop owner's wife – picking him up and carrying him off by force. Someone orders her to get out of there, get out of there right now, go find the beast, get out of the way if she doesn't want someone to kill her then and there, at least disappear until that poor woman knows her daughter is out of danger, that pregnant mother, the mother whose little girl's face has been destroyed and whose misfortune, it would appear, is all Nat's fault.

She shuts herself away in her house again, if it can even be called hers, even called a house. She doesn't have a choice, where else can she go? Wherever she might be, whatever she might say, she will be met with repudiation. Píter is the only person who comes to see her. He regards her with concern, narrowing his eyes. Nat is wrapped up on the sofa, staring blankly at the wall, pupils fixed. Píter tries to lift her spirits, but she only half-listens. The girl's injuries, it seems, weren't that serious, he says. She'll have scars, but there's always plastic surgery. Píter explains something about the cheeks, or one cheek in particular. Across from her, his own face is divided by a shadow. Nat only sees half of his countenance.

Píter looks much younger to her now, with his messy beard and cheekbones softened by the gloom, or maybe it's her, maybe she's aged and is seeing him from another era. His voice, low and soothing, continues to explain what Nat cannot grasp at the moment. How tiresome it is to listen when you have nothing to add, she thinks vaguely. Was this what happened to Andreas when she used to talk to him? Is this how her blather made him feel?

'Anyway, you should go out and offer to help. Ask how the kid is doing. She's only six, poor thing.'

'Poor thing,' Nat repeats. And then: 'It's not my fault.'

'No, of course it isn't.' Píter grabs her hand, gives it a squeeze.

'Everybody hates me now.'

'They don't hate you. But you need to cooperate. You can't refuse.'

Cooperating means handing Sieso over as soon as he turns up. To be put down. The dog – clever beast – ran away and still hasn't been seen since. Is he capable of understanding what he's done, of anticipating the consequences?

The men of La Escapa, accompanied by a couple of local police officers from Petacas, are scouring the area in search of the animal. They've made it as far as El Glauco and are prepared to climb to the top if necessary. The shop owner is the leader of the expedition. He is the most outraged, the most rabid of them all, as if his own daughter had been bitten. Nat can still hear the insults he slung at her. The gypsy husband was the only man who defended her. Leave the girl alone, he said. But then he joined the others in combing the fields.

The idea of putting the dog down horrifies her. She thinks that killing him will only deepen the tragedy. Not the girl's tragedy, not the girl's parents' tragedy, not even Nat's own, but the tragedy of the world in general, a kind of irreversible doom, as though the sacrifice of an animal – of that animal – would forever alter the order of things.

Píter is adamant. 'Don't you realize he's dangerous? That he could do the same thing to someone else?'

'She was the one who hopped the fence without permission and came in to play. Sieso wouldn't have attacked if she hadn't climbed over. Besides, where were her parents? Isn't it their fault for leaving her alone?'

Píter stands up, agog, scandalized.

'Don't say that! Don't you ever think about saying that to anyone! You're courting disaster!'

'More disaster?'

'You're in shock. You don't know what you're saying.'

Nat nods. She allows him to come close to her, cover her with a blanket.

'You need to rest. I'll come back tomorrow.'

The silence is different this time, theatrical, as if all of La Escapa was performing just for her, deception their singular aim. Everybody should be asleep, but there's no way anyone is sleeping. Nat imagines the men of La Escapa out looking for the dog. Looking for him with hunting rifles and sticks, stalking, ready to lynch him as soon as he's found. Are they going to kill him just like that, cruelly, paying him back for all the damage he has done? She dozes off, sinks into a feverish torpor. She dreams about torches, flames glittering, flickering in the distance. And she dreams about Andreas, his hands touching her, caressing her, appearing and disappearing. When she wakes, ochre light is seeping through the blinds. Several hours must have passed, although to her it feels like minutes. She hears a whine behind the door – a soft whine, gentle, almost human. Something is scratching at the wood. She leaps up, opens it. Sieso is on the threshold, looking her directly in the eyes. His coat is filthy and he has a new wound on his leg, but his gaze is clearer than ever. It's a miracle that he made it there without being seen. A genuine miracle, she thinks. Why kill such a creature?

They can't escape. The second she started the car engine, they would be intercepted – and she would be lynched, too. Even if she stays inside, goes days and days without showing her face, the moment they hear Sieso bark they will break the windows, break down the door like they did to the incestuous siblings, capture them in situ – there will be no escape. Like a cornered animal, she thinks, that's how they've got her. Like Sieso, who is still watching her and whimpering.

There's only one solution. Píter. He can help her. She can still try. She can convince him if she uses the exact right words, if she can convince him how important the dog's salvation is for them all – the entire community. She calls him on the phone and asks him to come as quick as he can, without revealing the reason to hurry.

Píter is struck dumb when he enters her house and sees Sieso there. His eyes swing between Nat and the dog, expectantly. Nat bursts into speech. Has he brought the car? Yes? He can take Sieso in secret, no one will suspect him. Drop him off at a pound. Or anywhere else, in another village. Go as far away as necessary. If the dog stays in La Escapa, they will beat him to death.

'You're crazy,' Píter interrupts.

But Nat keeps speaking. Imagine if it was his dog, she says. He wouldn't give it a chance to redeem itself? Even the most despicable criminal is afforded a defence. Has he forgotten what he told her about the snub-nosed adder? That all you had to do was move it away? She grabs him by the shoulders and shakes him. He's always said that he's her friend. Her real friend. He told her to come to him if she needed help. That's precisely what she's doing now. Why can't he support her?

'Because what you're asking me to do is insane. Not only is it not in your interest, it's to your detriment! You're upset and you don't understand. You'll thank me in time.'

Nat is enraged. Now he's rejecting her too? Is he aligned with the others, now that she's the weakest piece on the board?

'It's about safety. And justice. You can't fight it,' he adds.

Nat turns her back, looks away, orders him out of her house. Píter shuffles out. But he isn't the condemned one, she thinks, who does he think he is, walking like that, so dramatic? Surely, he must be satisfied now his predictions have borne out. That dog will only bring trouble, he said. It had sounded like a curse, and here is the result.

And maybe it is this correct prediction that gives Píter the authority to turn her in. It must've been him, since within the hour, two police officers are knocking on her door.

Nat can't stop them from taking Sieso. It's pointless to resist.

Joaquín comes to her door glumly, wringing his hands. Nat invites him in, but he would rather stay outside, not cross the threshold. With lowered eyes he tells her that it's better if she doesn't work for them for a while.

'At least until things calm down,' he adds.

Nobody would understand, he says. They get along with everyone, they have to avoid conflicts that could impact Roberta's health. Nat doesn't argue. She even admits that he's right. The dog bit the girl, the dog belonged to her, so she is guilty. It's justice. There's nothing more to say, nothing to discuss.

Joaquín apologizes again. The blush of embarrassment is visible on his cheeks.

'It's nothing against you. When all of this passes, you can come back.'

She sees Roberta that same evening, resting on the porch in the tatty striped deckchair where she usually gets her fresh air. The old woman signals for her to come near. Nat hesitates, she doesn't want to harm her or disobey her husband's orders, but finally she leans on the fence, just close enough to talk.

'Hey Roberta, how are you?'

Crossly, Roberta talks about her son. He promised he would take her to Italy, she says, but he forgot his promise. After she'd bought herself new dresses for the trip, she repeats, he forgot her. Nat knows they have a son who lives abroad whom they never see and hardly ever mention, but Roberta's speech doesn't sound all that logical.

'He got lost on El Glauco,' she says now. 'He got lost there, when he was little, before he had a beard. He had grass on his face, instead of hair.'

'That doesn't make much sense, Roberta.'

The woman looks away, as if hoping to change the subject.

'Who cares.'

Her hair is damp; Joaquín has probably just washed it and sat Roberta on the porch for it to dry. It looks nice that way, tucked behind her ears. Nat tells her so.

'You look very pretty, Roberta.'

'Why don't you come through and sit with me. I'm bored.'

'I don't have time right now. But I'm sure your husband would be delighted to sit with you and chat. Tell him.'

'Bah, he talks different. We never understand each other. Haven't you realized?'

'Realized what, Roberta?'

'That that man doesn't understand me.'

'You mean your husband? Of course he understands you!'

'No way. Here, in this place, no one understands anybody else.'

'Well, that happens everywhere.'

'Happens more in La Escapa, much more. Haven't you noticed that nobody was born here? Everyone comes from outside. Everyone speaks a different language. English, French, German... Russian! Chinese!'

Nat laughs.

'How can that be, Roberta? We all speak the same language here.'

The old woman tuts, waves her hand dismissively.

'Bah! You're so confused. See? You're not understanding me either.'

She can't forget Andreas. Her yearning is still immense. Sometimes her breasts swell with desire, her whole body tingles at the mere memory. His features, however, have already begun to blur. She shuts her eyes and tries to hold them, and yet they melt away. The sense of loss is swiftly gaining ground over her memory. She dreams about him again one night, but he is a taller man, more refined. In the dream, she dives into an unctuous calm. She makes easy strokes, contemplating the rays of sunlight sifting through the water, the greenish hue of a riverbed, the silvery shine of the rocks on the bottom. When she wakes, she thinks: no, that wasn't Andreas.

Another day, she thinks she sees him in the distance. The feeling is impossible to describe. Perhaps the closest thing would be like looking out of a window and viewing a scene from another world. A world that is now remote, painful and opaque. But wasn't that how it had always been: remote, painful, opaque? Yes, she thinks, but she was in it before; now she's outside.

She doesn't spy on him now – she would die if he ever caught her spying again! – but she observes his house from afar. The door is almost always closed – he used to leave it open – and the van is almost never outside. Where does he spend so much time?

An odd stillness surrounds his house, and is only altered by minute changes – the blinds up today, closed tomorrow, the wheelbarrow in a new spot, rain boots beside the door that disappear the next day – changes that demonstrate that Andreas is still alive. Somehow this fact surprises her, because she feels like he has already died.

What might he think about what happened, about everyone condemning her? Would he feel compassion? Or would he, like the others, believe she's guilty?

Everything has happened in a very short time. So short that she is astonished when she thinks about it. She opened a new tube of toothpaste when she arrived in La Escapa, a tube she has been using two or three times a day, and yet, almost a third is still left. It's incredible, she thinks: to be completely enlivened inside, shaken, spun around and around again, in less time than it takes to use up 125 millilitres of toothpaste.

One day, The Cottage gate is open. Nat gets over her reservations and goes to see how they are. The husband is by himself. He came to check on the house, he explains, and looks at her seriously, his expression closer to curiosity than reproach. He tells her that the girl is doing better, recovering. Nat asks if they are angry with her. When it's possible, she says, she would like to visit them. The girl and the mother, both. She wants to apologize in person. He thinks a while before he replies. He strokes his chin in reflection, a gesture Nat finds stilted. No, he says, they aren't angry with her. Carelessness was her only mistake. One can't go around adopting half-wild animals. Some risks cannot be tolerated, he repeats, and one doesn't have the right to take those risks without weighing the consequences. Nat would like to say that Sieso wasn't half-wild, that the man had liked him, that she even saw him petting Sieso once. She would like to defend herself, but she knows she has no right to a defence.

Looking at her, the neighbour's pupils oscillate slightly, as if scanning her. The truly painful thing for them, he continues, is that Nat didn't want the dog put down. They had lost a lot, their daughter had lost a lot, why had Nat refused to lose anything? She must understand it in those terms.

'But let's not talk out here. Come inside. It's cold.'

Nat accepts, although once inside The Cottage, the subject of the dog doesn't come up again. As he goes about switching on lights and turning on the heater in the living room, he talks to her about other things. He describes the minutiae of his job. He manages an insurance company, but his plan is to break away and open his own office. Being his own boss would be the best, he says, it's the only way to never be denied a raise! He laughs at his joke and then asks her about her own projects. He doesn't listen to her answer. And he doesn't seem all that worried about his daughter, Nat thinks, since his conversation is relaxed and he even looks happy. Maybe he's not all that upset, here with the not entirely unattractive neighbour girl, who he now has in the palm of his hand, thanks to the unpleasant affair with the dog.

She is in the palm of his hand, Nat repeats to herself, or one is in the hands of the other. There exists the possibility to buy and sell forgiveness, an apology, a

restoration of honour. He wields the power of the victim
and because of that privilege, he is, perhaps, the only one
who can intercede on her behalf. But in order to obtain that
pardon, Nat must expiate her guilt, surrender something in
return. Briefly, she delights in the idea. Why not? Wasn't
that how her story began with Andreas, an exchange of
goods? The neighbour clearly desires her. He has always
desired her and now he can attain her more easily than
ever. Nat imagines him licking his chops, closing in on her
like a wolf. She is suddenly overcome with disgust. Those
lips, that body, his weight on top of her, his sterile touch
emphasizing how far removed she is from what she had,
what she lost, what she can't manage to forget. It makes
her want to throw up.

The neighbour removes his jacket. Nat zips hers up,
says goodbye, and leaves.

A spirit of harmony spreads through La Escapa, symbolized
by the Christmas garlands the shop owners string on the
trees: little lights that blink rhythmically, a reminder that
the year is coming to an end and all must transform into
citizens of goodwill. Now nobody turns their head when she
walks past, there are no nasty looks or snubs, at least none
that she notices. At the shop, the girl goes back to treating
her naturally – if not quite the same as before – forgetting
or pretending to forget what happened. The gypsies offer
her a hound pup, assuring her the animal will never give her
any trouble, but Nat rejects the offer, terrified at the very
thought of giving it another try. Joaquín hints that she can
come back to their house whenever she wants – looking at

the floor, blushing when he says it. Even Píter apologizes. He didn't know how to handle the situation, he admits, he knows he let her down, but there'd been no easy solution, it was a hell of a dilemma.

Nat hopes that the return of the wife and the children next door will mean a return to normalcy, even if that normalcy is still a slippery thing. No transgressor can be absolved without receiving punishment first, but her break up with Andreas seems to have served that function for the inhabitants of La Escapa. Maybe they consider her expulsion from that state of inebriated happiness a harsh enough sentence. Would she be absolved, she wonders, if she was still wallowing like a sow with her lover, when the poor little girl still cries while having her dressings changed? Those, she believes, would be their words: wallowing, sow. Thanks to the fact that she has no lover with whom to wallow, Nat dares to come out of hiding.

She goes with Píter to Gordo's bar on Christmas Eve, where a few people have gathered for drinks. The night passes quickly; they eat heartily, joke, pop champagne, and sing carols. The girl from the shop gets drunk and dances on a keg, obscenely swinging her hips. Her father, also drunk, makes her get down, laughing his ass off. Nat feels like that night everything is allowed, everything is forgiven, even the old grudge between Gordo and the shop owner. And so she keeps an eye on the beaded curtain in the doorway, turning to look every time someone walks in. She is intoxicated with turbid hope, an effect of the alcohol. And what if Andreas comes? Her hearts races at the mere possibility. But Andreas does not come.

In the wee hours, confused and emotional, she exchanges goodbye hugs with the others, warm hugs in the cold night. On her way home, she is tempted to go by Andreas's. Just a little look, from a distance, she tells herself, there's nothing wrong with a little peek. Will he or won't he be home? Will there be a light on? Will music be playing? Will he have company?

But when she turns onto his road, the dark silhouettes of the prickly pears – sinister, threatening forms – make her turn back, like a warning.

She's returning from grocery shopping when she sees the neighbour woman in the doorway of The Cottage, watering the potted flowers. She stops in her tracks, laden with bags, her heart palpitating. When she starts walking again, the air is in such short supply that she can barely move forward. She knows she must go right over and say hello, but she advances slowly, discarding the words she must not utter, selecting more appropriate ones instead, all with the same care she used to take while translating, although now she doesn't know the meaning of the original text.

The neighbour greets her with a smile, pretty in a mustard-coloured sweater and wide-legged maternity pants, hair pulled back, gleaming cheekbones. Her attitude surprises Nat. That reception, she thinks, but she doesn't know how to finish the thought. That reception.

They exchange kisses on the cheek. Nat's voices breaks when she asks after the girl. The neighbour says she's doing much better. She calls the girl so Nat can see her and the child obediently emerges from the back of the house.

Despite its length, the wound that bisects her cheek hasn't disfigured the child's features, which are extremely delicate and still undefined. There are also a few smaller marks on her chin and neck. But it's her seriousness that is most striking. She looks at Nat with expressionless eyes.

'They told us that the scars will barely be noticeable with time,' the mother explains. 'The lucky thing about being a child. The skin regenerates wonderfully.'

Nat tears up. She apologizes to both of them. If only she could turn back time, she says. She is so terribly sorry for the damage she caused. So terribly sorry, she repeats. The girl is unmoved. The neighbour puts a reassuring hand on her arm and steps aside so Nat can come in. Nat enters their house, still holding her bags. Bewildered, she sits where she is told and looks around for the husband, the little boy.

'They're not here,' the neighbour says. Nat hasn't asked.

Then she offers her coffee. While she prepares it in the kitchen, the girl remains at Nat's side, standing in silence. She has the vague stare of a child without a past; her eyes, more than the scars, now mark the existence of a before and after, a glitch in time. Nat tries to chat with her, but the girl answers in monosyllables. The child's own verdict, set in stone, is consolidated in her expression. She has read Nat her sentence, and it is not favourable.

'She's very introverted,' the neighbour says when she returns.

They talk about her pregnancy, about Christmas. How was the Christmas Eve party? Did they have fun at Gordo's? They had to be with their families, obviously – her parents and his mother – the grandparents miss the grandchildren, but now, these days, she feels like retiring to the countryside. She's planning a little outing, Nat can come if she wants. Nat is uncomfortable. What is the meaning of this kindness? She has trouble chatting as if nothing's happened, but she thinks it is what they expect of her, and she must try. Now the neighbour is talking about costs. The cost of doing the renovations – the pool project, but also the kitchen, which has to be completely redone – plus Christmas presents, heating, medical expenses... Nat catches on. It hadn't even occurred to her. She isn't sure if the woman said it in passing or purposefully slipped it into the conversation, but she swallows and asks:

'Was it... a lot of money?'

Oh, no, the neighbour hurries to explain. She means the pregnancy expenses. She sees a very prestigious OB-GYN, the same one who did her other deliveries, one mustn't skimp on some things. The girl's treatment was covered by insurance. Fortunately, she adds, Nat doesn't have anything to worry about. The past is in the past. She comes closer, leans in a bit, and lowers her voice. As she speaks, she traces the rim of her mug with a fingertip, taking the time to enunciate each word.

'Look, if we'd wanted to fuck you over, we would have reported you.'

Nat freezes, unable to react. That manner of speaking, suddenly, is like a backhand across her face.

'What?'

'Report you. I'm saying we could have reported you. And we didn't. If we had wanted to fuck you over, fuck you over good, we would have done it, because you had everything to lose. So, you see, we have no intention of getting you back. You can relax.'

Baffled, Nat nods. She can't interpret whether the neighbour's smile disarms or accentuates the aggressiveness of her words: a tight smile exposing her magnificent teeth. Her eyes move to the girl, who has sat down on the floor, in a corner. She's playing a video game, supposedly cut off but – it seems to Nat – not missing a beat of the conversation. The neighbour changes the subject, her smile softens almost imperceptibly, and now she talks about her husband. He went to the grocery store in Petacas, she explains, it's getting harder to find what you need in the shop. What she said just a few minutes before now seems like the product of Nat's imagination, and yet she knows it's not, it had been a piece of the staging all along: a meticulously studied script, performed line by line. Nat no longer hears, she wants to get out of there, but she doesn't know how to end it. The neighbour rambles on, leaning back in her armchair. Occasionally, the girl looks up from her device, examines them seriously, and returns to her game. An excuse occurs to Nat. The heater, she murmurs. She left the heater plugged in. She'd better get going, she adds, it's an old model, it could catch fire any minute.

At the door, the neighbour takes her by the shoulder. This time she says Andreas, not the German, like she used to call him. Andreas, point-blank.

'I'm glad he left you.'

Her eyes gleam as she says it. Nat wants to protest, wants to ask where she got her information, but she limits herself to a smile. The stupid smile of a clown, she thinks: the girl's injury gives her mother the legitimacy to act like this, the right to keep assaulting her, like someone bursting into another person's home. Andreas has a dark character, the woman tells her, manipulative and dirty. She knows him very well. Very well, she repeats, and those two words grow large: they contain a whole language, a whole private, secret world to which Nat has lost access. Nat could remind the woman that she'd said just the opposite once, that she hardly knew him. She could ask for details, she could wait to leave and try to understand. But the desire to flee, to get away, prevails. She grabs her bags, smiles again, and leaves without a backward glance.

As she puts the groceries away in the fridge, she finds several broken eggs and two yogurt containers, open and empty. When had that happened? Who did it? She doesn't recall having left the bags unattended for even a minute. That – the broken eggs and empty yogurts – disturbs her more than the rest of the scene.

The landlord turns up on December 30th in a bad mood. The first thing he tells her, muttering at the floor, is that they've charged him double the usual price for a baby goat. They take advantage of everybody – idiots, all of them – who want something special for dinner on New Year's Eve, he's sick of their nerve. Sick, he repeats. Nat feigns indifference and goes to get the money. Who cares if it's New Year's, the landlord says, taking a seat on the sofa. If it were up to him, they'd eat a kettle of crisps and drink a few litres of beer, and call it a night. But the women, he says, they're the ones who complicate everything, obsessed with celebrating special dates, anniversaries and birthdays, showing off with their dishes, as if the food wasn't going to be shat out in the end anyway. He wipes spittle on his sleeve, gives Nat a lengthy, mocking smile, and asks about the dog.

'Guess he was a real dud, eh?' he laughs.

It was her fault, he says, for not knowing how to handle him. Dogs aren't that complicated, they just need a firm hand. She spoiled him with her whims, with that nonsense of bringing him to the vet – or does she think he doesn't know about that? Whims on the one hand, and on the other, that obsession with tying him to the stake. Not surprising the dog went nuts. In any case, it's too late for regrets, every dog has his day. Still seated, he digs around in his pocket and hands her the bills, folded and wrinkled.

Nat does her calculations, gives him the money. He counts it slowly, leery. He stands up to observe her, legs spread, fists on his hips. She holds his stare until she buckles and lowers her eyes.

'And what are you going to do here now?'

Nat doesn't answer. She just wants him to leave.

'Now that you're not screwing anybody, I mean, what are you doing here?'

Something pops inside her. Like a sac of cold gel that spreads through each one of her limbs and extremities, weakening her muscles, annihilating her. She steps backwards.

'Or maybe you are screwing somebody. When there isn't one, there's always another. Isn't that right? Anybody will do.'

He comes closer. Nat backs up until she is against the edge of the table. She tries to scuttle farther away, but he holds her by the arm.

'Come here,' he whispers. 'Don't you want me to give you a little something too?'

Nat wants to cry out but her terror prevents it. Before she can make a sound, he claps a hand over her mouth as the other grips her arm even harder. He puts his head against hers, whispers in her ear.

'Don't scream. Nobody is coming to help you.'

She tries to get him off her, pushes at him as hard as she can, but the landlord shows surprising resistance, trapping her, pressing against her, his body sweaty, enraged, hard and stinking, controlling her, slamming her into the wall, twisting her arm as he commands her to shut her mouth, threatening to tie her up and gag her if she doesn't behave.

'Come on,' he says. 'Don't be a prude. You fucked the German and the hippie. You fucked your neighbour, maybe you even fucked the old man whose house you clean. Do I deserve any less?'

Holding her against the wall, he grabs her by the hair, forcing her head back. She feels a wrench of pain, his slobber on her neck, on her breasts, his growl as he subjugates her. She shouts, but what leaves her covered mouth is not a cry for help: her strangled voice, stripped of its humanness, is the squawk of a bird before slaughter. He pulls her even more tightly, crushing her with his weight. Then he steps back, spits to one side, and laughs loudly.

'You're in luck, girl. Suddenly, I'm not in the mood.'

Nat contains her retching. She finally screams. She shouts that she'll call the police, she's going to report him, she'll tell everyone what he's done.

'Oh yeah? Will you tell your neighbours? Think they'll come to your defence? Why do you think I'm here?'

Sore, taken aback, Nat cries, rubbing her neck and bruised arm. She orders him to leave.

'Well 'course I'm leaving. Didn't think I was going to rape you, did you?'

Then he says that she makes him sick. He'd choose any woman over her. A she-goat, a cow. With her señorita airs, he says. Those flat tits and that bean face. Go ahead, report him if she dares. No one will believe her, there are no witnesses. If she reports him, her neighbours will do the same to her. Or did she think the matter of the dog was closed? They still have time, if they want to. He doesn't care what she does. She should stop her bellyaching.

He runs two fingers – the middle and index fingers together, held stiff – along the edge of the table as he stares her straight in the eye. That touch lingers even after he's left and is starting the Jeep, and even a little later, coagulating in the air.

Nat does not call the police. She doesn't call anyone. She sits on the floor and drinks straight from a bottle of whisky Píter brought one day. She seeks respite in numbness. But the roots of her hair still hurt from being yanked. And spasms wrack her hands.

She wakes with a sharp pain hammering her brain. Daylight wounds her eyes. How long has she slept? She blinks hard, once, twice, several times, becoming aware of the room, the moment, and herself. She stumbles to her feet, tripping on the furniture. She sees herself from the outside, from a position of false calm, like someone filming her, an extra, an interloper, the most insignificant role that could be assigned in a fictitious world – a set made of plastic, of cardboard. She drinks greedily but the water does not quench her thirst. She speaks out loud to clear the huskiness in her voice. Coughs. Her throat stings. It's cold.

She puts on her winter jacket and goes outside. The sun is already high in the sky, but it provides no warmth. More fakery, she thinks. A painted sun, rubbish. The sky is stretched taut over El Glauco, the road stretches before her, marking the direction she must take.

Andreas's van isn't outside, but this time Nat doesn't stop to spy from a distance. She goes up to the house and sits beside the front door. She stays there for several hours, indifferent to whether the others can see her, indifferent to what they say about her, the rumours they spread, the accusations she receives or the offences they allege, and absolutely indifferent to her dignity – or what, in other times, she would have called dignity but is now just an elusive term. She pees outside, in the bushes. She snuggles into her coat, reclines as best she can, dozes on and off.

She spends the whole day on the doorstep.

On the edge of night, the sound of an engine plucks her from her torpor. She sees the van first and then Andreas, getting out. She stands, smooths her hair. He looks at her wordlessly. Unmistakably severe. She has trouble recognizing him. Was that what his eyes were like? His body?

Wasn't he a little taller, or shorter, maybe? So hunched, so thin? She goes to him and lays the palm of her hand on his chest, no pressure, just barely touching him, an acknowledgement. Beneath the fabric, Andreas's skin releases a gentle heat, real and undeniable. But even that warmth doesn't remove her from the stage set, from the sense that none of this is real.

'Why did you come?'

'I don't know.'

It's true: she doesn't know.

He observes her with curiosity. He looks closely at her bruised neck. Maybe he can guess.

'You don't look so good,' he says. 'Come on, come in.'

Inside, the house is warm and smells of firewood. Nat sits on the sofa and looks around in the half-dark, floundering in the strange mix of recognition and unfamiliarity. Li comes over, purring, and rubs against her leg. Now they are both confused: Nat is unsure of her next step and Andreas, clearly, expects something from her, expects her to say or do something: why else is she there?

But it's evident that Nat has nothing to say to him. She studies him carefully, as if studying a stranger, while he takes a pack of cigarettes from his pocket, lights one, and smokes in silence. Who is that man? Why has she spent hours on his doorstep, waiting for him? What was the point, now that this paralysing chill has settled within her?

Months ago, he asked if he could be inside for a little while. Now it's like she is asking it of him, though in a different way. The man before her had ignited something inside her, something big and unknown, labyrinthine and inexhaustible, yet she feels nothing. A message had once flickered in Andreas's eyes, a message she had interpreted as access to power or insight beyond other people's reach. But that's gone.

Maybe she got carried away by greed, the selfish urge to grab more than was hers to take. Maybe it was true and she was ungrateful. She had touched God, and still, it hadn't seemed enough.

Andreas breaks the silence. With a passionless calm. He knows everything that's been going on lately. Everything? Nat asks. Yeah, everything. But she'll get through it, he assures her. She shouldn't torture herself over what people say. Nat feels the weight of distance in his words.

'You know? I had to go to Cárdenas recently. Armed cops in the streets. Everything cordoned off, helicopters circling. They were waiting for somebody important, a prime minister, I think, a head of state or something, for some international summit. I didn't wait to find out, I left as soon as I could. A horror show.'

Nat doesn't react. She doesn't understand what Andreas is saying. What is he talking about? Is he trying to comfort her, or warn her about a danger? Is there a hidden message in his words? Or is he just trying to take her mind off things? He sounds artificial, as if someone else was speaking for him, or through him.

In truth, he sounds ridiculous, clumsy, uneducated, just like he had seemed to her at first, when she saw him from afar and he was just a piece of the landscape, nothing more. The German, an ordinary man, a man like any other. And she, Nat thinks, she had been set on translating him, on bringing him to her territory. What an absurd ambition. It would be funny if it wasn't so ludicrous.

'What are you laughing at now?' he asks, stunned. 'I just don't get you at all.'

She considers staying, for a time. But the opposite urge – to leave – weighs on her as well. She doesn't need to disprove anything. She isn't looking to contradict anyone or draw attention to herself. But she wants to complete what she started and left half-finished. She doesn't want to give in. The translations of the theatre pieces, for example. Among other things.

Eventually, she decides to go live in a town nearby. She rents a very old house for less than what the landlord in La Escapa charged her. She washes the floors, scrubs the burners on the stove, sweeps and rakes, varnishes old wood, scrapes the old tiles clean, prunes dead branches: she doesn't consider it stagnation, the repetition of the same chores in a new place. To her, it's progress. Every now and then Píter comes to see her, bearing gifts. He is as attentive as he was in the beginning, if not more so. His attentions no longer bother her. The two of them, she thinks, are more alike than she thought. Píter, at least, talks.

She feels invincible, beyond judgement, but her immunity comes from having lived, for a time, as if climbing an endless staircase; she tripped on a broken step and fell into a void while the rest of the people kept climbing up and up, never noticing.

Something still twists in her gut when she thinks about Andreas, like a hangover. She often closes her eyes and finds comfort in the memory of his hands running down her sides. The first touch of his fingers on her waist. The T-shirt that accentuated the rest of her nakedness. The darkness silhouetting the shape of their bodies. The plink of raindrops on the metal roof. She thinks about how a single instant – that instant, for example – is enough to justify an entire life: there are people who never had even that. But other memories have lost their substance. She discards them one by one, until she is left with nothing except that first day.

Her memory has shrunk. Her memory, now, is so small that it fits in her fist. Sentimental relics, she tells herself, don't deserve eternity.

One day she takes the car and returns to La Escapa. She drives up El Glauco and parks at the lookout point where she and Andreas left the van. She follows their exact same route, not to revive the same emotions, but to erase them and write new ones on top.

Seated on a rock, she admires the scenery, the glassy film cast by the clouds, the wash of diluted colour. She inhales slowly. The chill air clears her nose, stinging a bit. Without meaning to, she composes an impromptu, private farewell.

She feels a tickle on her hand, an ant. She discovers a line of them, marching across the rock where she sits, a disciplined line except for the specimen that crawled over to her hand: the wayward one, the renegade.

She observes the ants closely. It's hard for her to reconcile the broad view from the top of El Glauco with that narrow universe: the large and small, all together on the same mental plane.

She achieves a kind of peace, a revelation. Unexpectedly, the theft she committed in the past gains all its significance. She now knows how to read it.

She understands that it isn't by aiming that one hits the mark, but randomly, by way of swerves and roundabouts, almost by chance.

She sees clearly how everything has led to this exact moment. Even that which didn't seem to lead anywhere.

THE PEIRENE SUBSCRIPTION

Since 2011, Peirene Press has run a subscription service which has brought a world of translated literature to thousands of readers. We seek out great stories and original writing from across the globe, and work with the best translators to bring these books into English – before sending each one to our subscribers, six to eight weeks ahead of publication. All of our novellas are beautifully designed collectible paperback editions, printed in the UK using sustainable materials.

Join our reading community today and subscribe to receive three translated novellas a year, as well as invitations to events and launch parties and discounts on all our titles. We also offer a gift subscription, so you can share your literary discoveries with friends and family.

A one-year subscription costs £38, including UK shipping. International postage costs apply.

www.peirenepress.com/subscribe

'The foreign literature specialist'

The Sunday Times

'A class act'

The Guardian

PEIRENE | STEVNS
translation prize

The Peirene Stevns Translation Prize was launched in 2018 to support up-and-coming translators.

Open to all translators without a published novel, this prize looks to reward great translation and to offer new ways of entry into the world of professional translation.

The winner receives a commission to translate a text selected by Peirene Press, the opportunity to spend two months at a retreat in the Pyrenees and a dedicated one-on-one mentorship throughout the translation process.

The Peirene Stevns Prize focuses on a different language each year and opens to submissions from October to January.

With thanks to Martha Stevns, without whom this prize would not be possible.